3/91

4/09 only 5y—
20x
3 since 04

by David Bromige

The Gathering (1965)
Please, Like Me (1968)
The Ends of the Earth (1968)
The Quivering Roadway (1969)
Threads (1970)
Three Stories (1973)
Ten Years in the Making (1973)
Birds of the West (1974)
Tight Corners & What's Around Them (1974)
Out of My Hands (1974)
Spells & Blessings (1975)
Credences of Winter (1976)
Living in Advance [with de Barros and Gifford] (1976)
My Poetry (1980)
P-E-A-C-E (1981)
In the Uneven Steps of Hung-Chow (1982)
It's the Same Only Different / The Melancholy Owed Categories
     (1984)
You See, Parts 1 & 2 [with Opal Nations] (1986)
Red Hats (1986)
Desire: Selected Poems 1963-1987 (1988)
Men, Women & Vehicles: Prose Works (1990)

DAVID BROMIGE

MEN, WOMEN
AND
VEHICLES
PROSE WORKS

BLACK SPARROW PRESS
— SANTA ROSA — 1990 —

ACKNOWLEDGMENTS

While the major portion of this material is new and unpublished, there are pieces which have appeared previously, sometimes in versions since emended. I wish to thank the editors and publishers of these books and journals in which such pieces previously appeared: *Three Stories* and *Tight Corners* (Black Sparrow Press), *Ten Years in the Making* (New Star Press), *My Poetry* (The Figures Press), *In the Uneven Steps of Hung-Chow* (Little Dinosaur Press), and *The Falcon, Gallery Works, Jimmy & Lucy's House of K, Kaimana, Meanjin Quarterly, Poetry Review* (London), and *This.*

"One Spring" owes much to *The Sebastopol Times,* especially to Vinson Brown, writer of a column called "Exploring Sonoma County"; there are borrowings also from Turgenev and Conrad. In 1980, a slightly different version was reprinted in that year's *Pushcart Anthology.*

Black Sparrow Press books are printed on acid-free paper.

LIBRARY OF CONGRESS CATALOGING-IN-PUBLICATION DATA

Bromige, David.
    Men, women & vehicles : prose works / David Bromige.
    p. cm.
    ISBN 0-87685-797-7 (paper) :   — ISBN 0-87685-798-5 (hardcov) :
  — ISBN 0-87685-799-3 (signed hardcover) :

    I. Title. II. Title: Men, women, and vehicles.
PS3552.R635M46   1990
813'.54—dc20   90-1061
                                     CIP

for Cecelia, the Belle who tolls for me

These stories are works of fiction and any resemblance between the characters and persons living or dead is purely coincidental, except for G. P. Skratz.

Contents

DOWN FROM THE MOUNTAIN

AUTHOR'S P.S.

MEN, WOMEN & VEHICLES: PROSE WORKS

Author's Note

for R.G.

I'm leaving the freeway in San Rafael when I hear this siren and think O shit, another speeding ticket. I see the other cars slowing down though, so maybe it's a fire or an ambulance. I start to pull over myself (to the left curb; it's a one-way street) when I hear this motorbike behind me. But it's riderless; just this empty bike rolling along and running up on the sidewalk and falling over with wheels spinning.

Everyone else has cleared out so I stop, get out to investigate. The engine's still running—and there's a package on the back with a piece of paper with an address written on it. So I get aboard the bike and set off to find the place. It's like the bike has a will of its own; all I have to do is sit on it and grip the handlebars to be taken there. By now I'm convinced I'm mixed up in something criminal and worry that I am erasing vital prints from the handlebars, but figure whoever was on it before probably wore gloves; anyway, does rubber retain prints?

It's a place like a kindergarden but the officer (he's not in uniform) tells me it's a temporary police station. He thanks me for bringing the bike and the package on the back, which he opens: it's like an expensive stereo radio—and he tells me: "We're getting more and more of this sort of crime out here now, too, like in Miami." (I remember reading words to this effect in the paper a month or so back.) "Meaning Wars. People import shipments of meaning and there's a big market for that stuff here in Marin. As though people here didn't have enough to distract them already! The dude who rode this bike probably got offed by a rival gang. It's death to sell meaning below the going rate." He goes on to tell me that the stuff is highly addictive, and that on the street it's often adulterated, and that the legislature will never legalize it for fear of losing control over the electorate. All the time he's telling me this there's a bustle of people, teachers I suppose, and kids, and help (people who serve up the hot lunch) coming and going around me in this large room with tiny tables and chairs painted in bright primaries. It's like a school but it's also like some command post during a battle. I wonder whether I'll get a citation. I haven't been asked to fill out any forms—no paperwork is being done; it's all highly irregular. This guy is too laidback to be a real cop, even in Marin.

He shakes my hand and asks one of his "men" to drive me back to my car. The person in question looks foreign to me, and doesn't speak much English. He says, "St. Paul?" I get into my car and drive to Minneapolis.

COMING OF AGE IN THE FIFTIES

Barscene, Oakland, '59
(We're All Dead Now)

Fasttalking character looks like Fred Astaire circa 1953 jollying along elderly woman drunk ("lady") who is trying to play piano. His cuffs are deep, long, and stretched like hardwood. He wears patentleather dancepumps. (He knows he looks like Fred Astaire.) She rejoins oldish man ("better preserved") at one end of the bar. Orders. The bartender (John Diefenbaker, Premier of Canada, circa 1958) brings a gin-and-something, though the man she's with disapproves. In comes a middle-aged couple. Fred greets them effusively is an understatement. Woman has rags of attraction clinging still. Man is older, redfaced. So's Fred, now clearly drunk.

"Have somethin special, a Scotch Mist'sa kinda martini."

"No thanks," the woman says, rather stand-offishly.

"Know you're thinking we don't know one nother very well. Let me rememdy that. Let me at least show you some aspect of myself, which I choose to present. As though I wanted to sell you something."

Hard to believe one's ears. The new arrivals settle for something less intimidating than Scotch Mist, take a table, sit and attend to Fred.

"Been disputin the name of this tune with Reena." He indicates the woman at the end of the bar, dances over to the piano, plays "In the Mood." Dances back.

He's anxious the couple should be aware that he knows a Mr. Goldschmidt, a solid citizen of San Jose. Unlike Goldschmidt's brother, a delinquent whom Fred likes to talk about.

The old woman at the bar asks the barkeep Fred's name.

"Johnny Steiner, S-T-E-I-N-E-R."

Waveringly, she expresses her admiration for Johnny.

Johnny meanwhile is saying, "It's not one of your new rest homes, the house is 100 years old, but it was built so magnificently that you go through it, it's all THERE. Sue has a license. It's a rest home, it's a nursing home. Old people, tired of looking after themselves, sell out everything and move in with us. Sue."

Down the bar, the old woman can't pay for her drink. Barkeep quietly aggrieved, woman plaintive. Barkeep walks away, leaving the matter of payment up in the air. It seems the old man has some money but won't give it to her.

"Was going to bring you a dozen red roses," he growls, "but now, damned if I am."

"Can't I have jus' one more drink, on my birthday?"

"No. You made a fool of me on the piano. Let's see how you like being lonely. I'm moving out."

"After all, jus' one drink? After all, 'smy money?"

"Is it bedamned. I worked for it, wouldn't you say? Damned right I did! *Your* money!"

She doesn't answer. Meanwhile he repeats "is it?" again and again. He could be twisting her wrist.

The barkeep asks Johnny to play some boogie. Johnny protests extravagantly. But it isn't quite the protest of the man who's dying to be asked. That's there; Johnny clearly knows that tone; but there's resentment too.

"After all, you're the boss."

Maybe Johnny does work here. He dashes off "In the Mood" again, dances back to his companions. From the bar, the old woman calls to him to play "I'll See You in My Dreams."

"Only if you sing."

Then, hastily realizing she's drunk enough to take him up on this, adds, "And I don't think I could keep in key right now. . . ."

Then he gets carried away: "I have to be *in* a pretty funny *mood* to play that one, and, well, I'm in a funny mood now," his companions laugh, the barkeep laughs, "but not in the same way. Anyway, my friends and I must be on our way."

Great protestations of friendship towards the barkeep. Each wants (he or she says) to know if the other will be back this evening. No one sounds sure, but says emphatically he, she will be.

"Well, here we go, we're off for dinner and things." Johnny makes it sound like Top of the Mark. But it's probably not even as fancy as Jack London Square.

The old woman gets up and tries to play "I'll See You in My Dreams." As she crosses to the piano, the barkeep goes down the bar and stands by the old man.

"Jeezus Christ." The old man says this.

The old woman begins to sing.

Coming of Age in the Fifties

They wanted to give him all of it, he thought. But maybe their wide open faces were impossible for them to live up to. Why wouldn't they give it away. All of it. Back? Hardly. At this time few Indians seemed to care. Were they waiting, with the patience hopefully attributed to them, for all of it to vanish like the heat-mirages out along the blacktop? The Old Timer had never tired of recounting his hardships. Why hadn't he quit? Loner had walked clear into it. Well, I'll tell ya, it's like having a wildcat by the tail. That was the poker-game exactly. He was to be given all of it, but slowly, for time is space when both get wide enough. Still, Loner couldn't deny he felt he had only just sat down, six o'clock, cold sober, empty ashtrays, I must empty these ashtrays he told them. They growled, as he left, glad of the opportunity. But for what, he wondered.

The women hushed like a church as he entered the kitchen. I'll take them, one said, affronted. None of them was his. Smiling, he pressed past them all and at the second attempt, locked the door. The liquor and the mix pressed hard on his bladder and he closed his eyes with the relief. However, he found he couldn't, so hampered, master his direction, the pee was going straight into the water so that the women couldn't help but hear. Opening his eyes he found one of them regarding him. I'm in here, he said. She motioned to him that he was to think nothing of it and perched herself on the edge of the tub to get a closer look. The wind that all along had been buffeting the house now came to his attention. Had it blown the door open? Nice, she said, her face came closer. A house, bereft of company, across a thousand baldheaded miles, came to attention. Lightning flickered along the eaves. He could no longer see the Welcome on the mat as she grabbed him by the balls. Two staples gleamed in her fold. I love you, Loner said. Ding Dong, she chortled. It was time to take a shower and this he did, striking a few poses for her amusement.

Going back through the kitchen, he staggered, and put his hand out to steady himself, against the buttocks handiest. Watch it buster, their mistress said, frowning, faces of disapproval all round, I bet he jerked off in there, the dirty thing. Oh, they never get enough, I know the type. Men! said the one with the staples. They're all the same. Out for what they can get. General agreement.

Figgered you fell in, said Real Estate. I took a shower, Loner told them. Ain't you got no shower at home, said the other, leaping to the next possibility. The Kid cackled, He ain't got no home. Loner saw how that was true. They understood him, these Men. Maybe he was one of them. However he had a small apartment, and stood up once more. Siddown. Real Estate had reached the third and final leg of the evening, of any evening. Loner complied and picked up the hand they had dealt in his absence, preventing his hand from shaking by the simple expedient of grasping its wrist with the other hand. He was told the call was 3 thirty 3. He found he had 5 of a kind. When time came to show them as he drew his winnings in he met a look of assumed bafflement in Real Estate's face. At last the chips were down. I called this one, the huge man said, with huge deliberation. And what I called was, *not* what you thought it was. Loner had never seen a room with fewer doors—or windows, come to that. Even the hot-air vents had heavy grilles across them. Bull sheet, not Loner but the Kid drawled, going for the bottle with his teeth. The Kid moved fast, but Real Estate moved faster, and Loner perceived he had served his purpose. The other two men, whose names he had never quite caught, joined in with heavy joy. The furniture began to come apart with a labored dexterity that suggested some method. There was no place for Loner to sit and figure out how it was done.

I just happen to be driving your way, let me get you home. Which one it was he couldn't, yet, tell. She snapped on the radio and attended with painful concentration his attempts to shout it down. I like this tune, she said. At last he was alone with a drunken woman in an automobile. A thousand baldheaded miles to park

in! This isn't the way home, he mouthed, Where are you headed.
Just to drive around, she screamed, heading the Dodge straight
down the tracks. At every intersection the poles were down and
the red lights swinging. They had a clear run.

He kept trying to see her face but her coat had fallen open,
under which, she was nude. Her pubic hair, he noticed, had been
airbrushed away. Weren't you in the bathroom, back there? There
is no bathroom back there and don't you forget it. What are you
looking at? When I get you out to the dump, I'm gonna eat you
alive. Take the wheel.

He slid across awkwardly. Now in the back seat, where he
watched her in the mirror, she began to drag all kinds of clothing
over her, a girdle, a huge bra of fence-wire, and finally a padlock
such as he had seen on one of the two town taverns after the owner
had once too often served beer to minors. She had him breathing
heavily now. I'm a free agent, she told him proudly. Real Estate
wouldn't be through with the furniture for hours. What sounded
and then looked like, a freight, bore down on them. I think we
can just clear it, she said. When they got to the dump, if they
did, he realized she would take a little key, and fling it gaily into
the garbage. Then he could hunt for it, while from the car she
called encouragement to him—Cold, Warm, No, Cold. His friends,
he remembered, would be coming from the other tavern, with
their flashlights and their 22's, to pick off the rats that swarmed
there. Marry me, he wailed, while the locomotive's headlight
revealed to him the Dodge approaching along the rails ahead.

Action Mating

But there is this image of the hysterical woman
[sic] on a roller-coaster screaming I just love it
don't you?
—Robert Duncan

Because she trusted him implicitly, she gave herself permission to flow with the moment. It was herself she didn't trust and thus tortured him with the reproach of being unfaithful.

He was as insane as the next person though better educated. He had fine flashing eyes, flaring nostrils and the cutest long, silky ears. She could tell from the outset that he had a commitment to the reasonable, and had been delighted to discover he clung to it with absolute monomania. Under her skin was one with under her thumb to them both. All they lacked was a language.

Take a piece of blue—a big piece. And now look what you've done—splattered red blobs all across it. Ah, but that was accident for you. He was true blue as far as she was concerned. He had accomplished this by turning himself into her, who didn't know where to turn, she hoped, next. "I love you and I know it's forever." But he had climbed onto the stage to say these words to two persons who were waiting for a third—not even sincerely, since these were two actors. Anything he said, she saw, and saw it as writing—mere words. Talk about literal-minded, she interpreted a hand up her skirt as a flashy piece of prose.

Fractal. Really? Sex and torture meet in the same problem, how to hang draw and quarter someone while burning them at the stake you are having them slowly impaled upon. There's the observer's viewpoint. Subjectively, there's no choice. She had to keep him alive in order to go on killing him. But only as long as he squealed. There was the true distraction craved.

What he got out of it, what was in it for him, was tormenting her with his dogged fidelity. He could beat the best of them with that. But is there anything to believe in apart from oneself? Speak louder, they can't hear you. We thank you for the nice sentences. The prize, however, isn't edible.

Uncle Ed

Waking an indeterminable number of hours later, but it is the same place, again. Like a huge, dimly-lit body. The odor of whiskey fills the room but possibly his own sweat puts it there. Has he sobered up while he slept? Standing, stumbles, but this could be the unaccustomed posture and activity. Has he driven the others from the house or are they innocently about their errands. Or he is, innocent. As far as they are concerned, they think of him, whatever, wherever. Suffering, they think of him, for doesn't he suffer. We will do anything to be sure, a friend writes, destroy all our tenuously-held happinesses or satisfactions to put the truth of our essential nature out there for all to see—he laughs. People place a ridiculous degree of faith in words. They want only the activity, talking on to try to forget what's out there. What's out there, he thinks, in the room.

Walking back from the store, he is reminded, as a youth crosses the road, turning to grin at him—a future friend perhaps?—of Luke. His lissome body is not quite visible, not tangible as it ought to be. He has not seen Luke for some weeks—well, days, say. Hours. Just a very little while ago, which accounts for the keen impression of his not being here, now. The youth has turned the corner. Grim, to grow old, in all youthful eyes, and be unwatched. He sets the nice new bottle on the counter, attempts to open it. And succeeds! He is still good for something in this world then.

And were the opposite the case, who to know it? Watch him as they might—and this was a different time, for the people were back in the house, which was why he was hiding upstairs—they could never gain quite sufficient proof of his incorrigible worthlessness. They would try to predict his actions from his thoughts as guessed from his words, but he, in doing nothing, would demonstrate the senselessness of all such activity. Other times, in that other life—strange to this one, as childhood is strange to being grownup—he had been competently active. But could they be sure of him on that account? This could be the way he blew that cover.

So now he was downstairs, the picture of geniality, surly though they were, or tentative, humoring him perhaps. Hoping he would pass out, even if on the carpet. They would see how he could carry his liquor. He set the bottle on the counter. He invited each in turn to drink with him. Anything was to be preferred to their conversation. The holes annoyed him—through which you could drive a hearse. Death rendered all their busy plans ridiculous. Away with care! Actually, he had become invisible. Somebody else, like in the song, had taken his place. And yes, somebody else had taken his place with Luke. He wept, copiously. It was incredible, how he himself had aged. No time had passed, really, not remarkably so. That is, he could hardly regard this punishment as earned. Even in this respect he was a freeloader. But there one is, or was, at the height of your youthful strength, filled with ineptitude, while aptitude visits old age only to mock. Next, what you went in terror of for so long, as if that might fend it off, took you anyway.

Given thoughts like these, life was very long, alone night upon night, the only relief provided by those who shortly prove themselves insupportable companions. He squinted. It was a calendar. He had managed to subtract a further five days from his allotment. Misery gripped him. The day appointed for ending this misery had jerked five days closer. He would be dead, having failed, and no one to know it. There were seven bottles beside his bed, six empty. No reason not to empty the seventh. There were so many more, in just that one store, so many more days, or nights. Or youths. And a betrayal in each one, like the mescal worm. But miraculously he felt fine. The alcohol improved his health, it was a too-little-understood paradox. Meet the enemy halfway—more than halfway! He would soon be of a mind, if not an age, to hold converse with the youth who had so lately turned the corner. They were, after all, interchangeable, youths and himself, youths and each other, one soul, one's hole, world without end, round the bend and up your friend.

If he didn't go to the party, he couldn't be put down at the party. He would go drunk and be its life and soul! But it was as yet too early, like the pig's tail. He looked out the window to see a task he had abandoned, some weeks since, or days, in the middle, so that the next step would always be there, whenever he chose to take it. The longer he let it wait, the less likely it was to get done. They would watch him admiringly when he worked out in his grounds, but they were more intense in their attentions when he let things run to rack and ruin. He gave them more, then, in letting things go, and it was unfair of them to criticize him therefore, when he took a little time away from his projects to drink. And when they drank with him, it was to get drunk themselves, or to make themselves feel good by trying to show him how to do it without going completely overboard. If no one was watching now, he could see through that trick, for it was their only way to catch him acting naturally, which they might do at any minute. As long as he drank tomato juice for his health, and topped it off with vodka from the bathroom cabinet, they could hunt high and low for liquor in his kitchen. It was an obvious ploy and they were sure to find him out. They would grow anxious again, worry, suffer and thereby enter into an identity with himself once more. But even so, none of them could touch him, really, any more than his alcoholic intake could damage his liver. The liver is an astonishing organ—laid out in a thin line it would stretch halfway across the continent, a virtually endless trip. Odd, really, that it should be bunched up into a vulnerable bundle. There was something wrong with God's plan. God hated people. But at least there was a God. How else would you know something like your best could never be good enough. He smashes things so that we can decide to pick up the shards or not. He keeps us human. And he gives us alcohol. An endless supply of it, inexhaustible as time, too much of it, use it up fast. They drained the ocean to stop the tidal wave, they used a man-made tidal wave. You can make anything tangible by dismissing what can't be touched, probably even loneliness. Impossible projects are the best.

FOUR BLIND I'S

Triumph & the Will

How hard it is to speak of the death of love, if that is the death, and the emotion, I do speak of, here. There's an almost interminable search for the right word. And what makes it so difficult if not an equal determination not to disclose to oneself what the right word is. No choice is possible. One leaps, so to speak, and if (as is probable) one leaps forward, one will always land on one's face. To speak at all, so confronted, is to ensure that one or the other possibility wins out. There'll be a loss, also, roughly equal to the gain. There's no time to lose then, and I must begin as best I can.

I would be absolutely clear, at the outset, on one point: I'm a man who doesn't always get what he wants, but possessed of such determination and will-power that, I believe, had I wanted to be President, I would have come close. Others, luckier by birth, have done no more. Once I got the scent of some thing or person who could enable me to realize my desire, no further hindrances were possible to me, and to this day I'm capable of pursuing a line of action long after most would have seen reason and gone home. It may not seem odd, therefore, that I tell of this, but we blunder into grace as a thief into a safe, and that's a story in itself.

Hilda wasn't the first person I loved, but neither was she the last, and I select our story, I suppose, with some notion of a median in mind. Let me add that, in returning that love as she did, she introduced me to a complication, angry as it made me, that even now I'm hopeful may recur.

She was only passing through the town where then I lived, and this alone was sufficient to arouse the will of which I speak. Could I contrive to fall in love with her, or couldn't I, before the week was up? Even—or especially—if she felt no attraction toward me? Her person I found attractive, which should have

31

helped, but then, how should it be otherwise. I knew what I wanted, while men will find beauty anywhere. But nothing brought the affair to a head more than Hilda's own will. By the second evening we were hopelessly desirous of going all the way, of finding ourselves utterly at one another's mercy; and she, after all, would be out of this place and into the safety of the next stop on her itinerary, as fast as the next plane could carry her.

I don't know if she was a virgin but I was, for the one girl who had taken pity on me before had bitten off more than she could chew, expecting no more than a casual roll in the hay where I was looking for something far more obtainable. This may be difficult to comprehend these days, but I see a terrible obscurity refused in contemporary relaxation. Naturally enough, then, when Hilda, in that actual hayloft, lay back, I knew what was wanted of me and let my will have its way, so that, if her tour-guide hadn't shouted that I was to bring her to the house right away, I don't know what might not have happened. It might have ended then and there. But his indignation, and that of the entire group, was impressive, so that for the rest of her stay a tacit understanding—call it an irrational terror—kept us within its limits, and the romance flourished. And I had time to think things through.

If we fuck, I thought, we'll get what we want, and although that won't be the end of it, our commitment will be absolute and permission thus granted to the least desire the other might in all reason be expected to fulfill. This outweighed the claim I sensed in the alternative, namely, that to abstain from the ritual admitting us to such commitment opened the way to a rarer kind of love, scorn her as I would.

She wrote from her next stopover, with less ardor than I should have expected, and sensing in what she said, and even more, in what she didn't say, the fulfillment I was bent on, I quit my job—by then as tedious as anything one can do with one hand tied behind his back—and joined her. There, on a rock covered with slippery moss, she granted me a happiness I've never known either before or since, wriggling from her jeans to receive me in a way so unlike my imaginings that I came almost at once, initiated into this mystery with a swiftness that left me numb. It was achieved. From here on in, however in memory I'd try to violate her actual response, her calm acceptance would win out over my fantasies. Since puberty, or before, something in me had longed for this moment with this person, and that is what we mean by Fate. And now I was satisfied there was no turning back. In fact we repeated the act once or twice before we parted, increasing our pleasure by the use of safes.

Hilda had topaz eyes, a face somehow all profile, hair, arms, legs—I will remember them all to my dying day, for who knows? this may be it. Against the vicissitudes of Chance there's only the human will, and if mine shows me those topaz eyes blurry with tears, this is more than the cat sees, for where are her kittens today? She cried because she had told me she loved me so much that she'd twice let me do something disgusting to her. Given the act was so repulsive to her, I was loved indeed, and in a way that assured me sooner or later she'd be able to look unflinchingly at what we had together in a way consonant with my own. And I could appreciate her duplicity, during the act (for if she kept herself to herself at such times, still, she hadn't actively rejected me); for I put it to myself that, if she couldn't be trusted at a time like that, she was hardly to be trusted now. Probably there'd been a pleasure taken in it which she was incapable of facing up to now.

But all reflection aside, she'd won my heart, and what time had we left for reflection? It was time for farewells—she was to fly back home tomorrow. Although I'd resolved never to let her go, I'd seen her ticket, and my distraction, trying to reconcile these apparently contradictory facts, caused me to act oddly. She'd just taken a shower, and, seeing her naked body next to the scales, I suggested she should weigh herself. Her refusal so surprised me that I grew insistent, but try as I might I couldn't push or lift her onto them. How ridiculous—what did she think to hide? It was already obvious she was a big girl. Later, I saw this was a lovers' tiff, and further evidence that we were lovers. I wouldn't go to the airport to see her off. Why prolong the agony. I had meant to go, but slept late. My subconscious knew what it was up to, and wisely exchanged the pain of parting for the pain of a small betrayal and the ensuing remorse. But after all, I'd seen an airport before, and I'd seen Hilda. How stupidly literal does one need to be.

She wrote once. I was chagrined to hear she wasn't pregnant, for I wanted some tangible form to grow from our relationship, heavy as it had been heavy. And too, I knew, I don't know how, that I had the makings of a real father. Still, I believe the real reason I didn't use a safe that first time, although there was one in my pocket all along, was that she'd have suspected my far-sightedness, with its demeaning implications concerning her powers of resistance, and that she'd have concluded from that that I was too clear-headed to be truly in love. Her contempt was not my object, or, if it was, my diffidence lost me that opportunity.

She said nothing in the letter concerning any infidelities. I took her blandness for dishonesty. Then, as if from nowhere, I was inspired to think that, after all, what was she to me? I saw that, if I didn't in fact love her, her letter would mean nothing to me. With this realization my strength returned, I was able to pick up the letter and re-read it several further times. I had to admit that, to an outsider, her prose was decidedly thin—how could one love such insipidity? Yes, but were it not for love, how would blandness make its way in the world. Instrumentality is everywhere, and I was relieved to find I had my part to play.

Hilda for now was out of reach, so I laid my plans. I had to save my fare, I had to find a job, I had to find a room. I did the last two and began to do the first. I settled back to make all I might of the next stage.

The mail came after I left in the morning so it was early evening before I could sort through the letters on the hallstand and find no news of Hilda. Each evening I hurried back to the boardinghouse and scooped up my mail and ran up the stairs two at a time to reduce by several seconds the anticipated moment, which I see I delayed by not looking for an envelope with her writing on it until I was safely in my room, the door locked. Well, none of us is perfect. This I did six days a week for two months, my faith was unshakeable. What use to live wholly for the future. If we are to get what we want, now is the only time.

I had to suppose she was ill—had had an accident, was crippled, had lost a leg or an arm, some toes at least. Such thoughts caused me pain, though not, of course, as much as they were causing Hilda, if there's anything to telepathy. Of all the possibilities, the one I most often had in mind was that she was paralyzed from the waist down. But as time went by, I saw others. Sometimes I thought I could sit in that room forever thinking about them but the excitement of getting the mail depended on being away during the day. And the job was a constant humiliation, and that too kept me occupied.

I could usually ignore my employer—he would speak harshly, as if my errors were deliberate, but right or not, I knew I was quitting soon, so little could mar my enjoyment of his censure, impotent as it had to be. I had no time to finish any task he urged me to begin, his upbraidings themselves being practically insurmountable interruptions. In my opinion he didn't have long to live. That's why he projected his sense of defeat onto me, but he wasn't really there at all as far as I was concerned, for I had my love to keep me distant. True, if I was lonely before, I was lonely now, so nothing had changed. But now I could think of Hilda, and every detail of our time together. One day I rose to my feet and began to kick everything in reach, in short order I'd smashed the place, for I'd always known that where there's a will, there's a way. It was that same evening I went over to Adrienne's for what she termed "solace." She worked at the same place, and I'd only been able to resist her by telling her how I'd sworn fidelity to Hilda. Perhaps, since this made our relationship so much like mine and Hilda's at this time, it was a kind of infidelity after all, but I can't extract much satisfaction from that conjecture. Still, if your reach doesn't exceed your grasp, why do the trees grow fruit out of our reach?

Adrienne was a sympathetic listener, laughing when I said that and similar things. And when I'd told her something of Hilda, she had to respect my constancy, seeing that she wanted the same for herself. Which all her protestations about loving me now and without future designs could only make plain. This law of opposites was beyond her in her simple-mindedness, but, slow as she was, she was bound to make some man satisfied, and I had to be careful around her. As I discovered when, after spending my last week in town on her floor—for my landlady had started to come on to me too—I found myself, on the final night, in Adrienne's bed. But that's another story, a story all in itself; and one very much like this, so I don't have to tell it here. It was enough, that I would have that to confess to Hilda, when we met.

I couldn't afford a plane ticket, so I took the Greyhound. What we cannot reach by flying, we must reach by limping, as I always tell myself.

A year had passed, and Hilda had grown some four or five inches, so she was now six feet or so; her wrists, that had been long with that vulnerability I find highly attractive, so that I'd fancy how she'd look, hung from a beam, were now much bonier, as though she *had* been. Her face had lost its bloom, and all in all, I found her ugly, pitifully so, and redoubled my efforts to act as though I were still under her spell. And in a sense I was. Consider my investment! To cut my losses now would be like cutting my fingernails or my hair.

So understandably I didn't for the first few minutes hear what she was saying. Which turned out to be that she had written me a second letter—upon receiving my last, that announced I was about to come to her—and she had sent it to the boarding-house. I suppose the landlady there destroyed it, in a jealous fit. And Hilda's letter had told me it was all over, she was engaged to somebody else. I saw almost at once that my love was to be tested as never before. I settled into my chair and gazed into her face. I was prepared to listen to her forever. Although I'm alone as I write of it, it's as though she sat across that table from me still, telling me what to put down. I lost her, true, but in the long run, what difference has it made? I am still capable of laying this story at her feet, or, if she won't open it, at her door. I take no credit for my strength of will. If it is stronger than love itself, surely it comes from the same mysterious place—for which I can't, somehow, find the right word. But if I could, wouldn't it lead to another, then another? There would be no way to stop. I was unable to stop with Hilda, and that naturally makes me not want to stop now.

Darkroom

My wife and I used to be photographers. That is a picture of us right there. We called that her soulful expression—that smile that's just beginning. If I thought of it as *ours*, she bore with my conceit. She was the nature photographer. I felt the groves and meadows had been done to death, but she argued differently. Once, she caught a hamadryad—on film, I mean—though that's as *caught* as anywhere, I think. If I can only locate that print, I'll let you see it, it has to be one of the most remarkable examples . . . or nothing. If I find it you can help me decide.

People were my portion. That's drawing the line too clearly, but we haven't much time. It'll do. Everyone on this island could tell you that—man, woman, child, I posed them all. Of course on an island it's easier to be sure you haven't missed anyone, than elsewhere. It's actually too neat a way of proceeding but something like it would have to be true, for me to talk at all. I have wanted to be a writer but I've always felt defeated almost before I began, by the nature of the materials, whereas each snapshot, however blurry, is particular.

We used to sit and talk, trying to discover how each of us began, began, I mean, to be interested in—to be, a photographer. I never believed her story. I suppose that's why I can't recall it, though I could tell you how she looked, telling it. My father was one and among my earliest recollections is the darkroom he would sometimes let me watch him working in. I can smell the hypo still—somehow the stuff we used, ourselves, hadn't that same odor. Sanctity, I called and call it. My mother would say, Father's at it again—in his inner sanctum; so my derivation made no more sense than, say, to suppose rectitude stems from rectum. My wife and I used to joke along these lines, asking each other to please pass the holy water, or to make some, please. I guess most couples have their secret speech and it seems pretty well meaningless to outsiders. Isn't that in part its function? We'd do it in company, at times, but our friends didn't object, rather I believe they took pleasure in seeing us happy together, for once.

She was such an imposing woman, yet always I felt she sought something essential to her well-being, in me. She was strong enough to make her way in the world without me, as I told her, often. I had to lean on her but what she got out of it, who can say. It must have been my sense of this inequity which made me so bitter towards her. I adored her—she became my principal subject, I shot her in every imaginable posture and light. Nights, when she was asleep, I'd take out the proofs and pore over each inch.

I'd had girlfriends before—how else should I have known her worth? Yet she was in a class by herself and made them all look pale. Somehow she subsumed every last one of them. They became not so much her forerunners, as misplaced postscripts to her, once we'd met. But I wouldn't see them forgotten and would study their pictures too, from time to time. One evening I pulled out this photo, mainly a seascape—it was early work—but containing, within its left-hand margin, a pair of hands. These caressed me once, I found I had said, aloud, the very day this was taken, these lavished their tenderness on this same person that now sits here. Those are various colored dots impressed on processed paper, she told me. I accused her of insane jealousy: insane, because this woman from the past had in fact made her own happiness possible. An expression of strained patience I had already come to detest suffused her features. Once is enough, she pointed out, and the truth is finer than all your fancies. That's a photograph. I should know. I'm a photographer.

A better one than me. Yet still she clung to me, and though the exchange I've just repeated might lead you to think otherwise, usually she would defer to me. Even when it must have been apparent to both of us that she knew best, she would yield, filling me with apprehension and, at least once, with terror.

This was during our first month of courtship. That term sounds odd, today, but she exuded an archaic quality that demands such dated speech at times. I remember us seated on the floor, in her apartment, after a day at the beach, I was explaining a novel attachment to her, when we heard them. They came nearer, footsteps, and I found I was saying, Shall I let them come in—it was a joke, all a pretense, it was only some passer-by, a nobody as far as we were concerned, walking home, late. No, she said, No, send them away, please, quickly, now.

I've said that hers was my strength—from the start. Giddy with the rush of belief in my powers I said, teasingly, but in deadly earnest, I can bring them in, if you want. They were very close now—about outside the window. Shall I. They faltered, paused. In a panic I never knew her in again she shouted No, send them away. They went on by and I knew in that instant that was what I had wanted all along. But didn't her belief require the alternative course? That's what I mean when I say she deferred to me.

A pattern was set—then, or maybe even earlier—whereby I spent our time together showing her things. I brought her to this island and among these people. I showed her, picture by picture, how her animation faded, how destructive my company must be, to her. In this occupation too she was an unflagging support. But she did grow tired more readily and then, her face sagging, dozing in a chair, I could think she was my father. Other times, striding by my side over her beloved moors, she was my mother, and listened avidly to what I could show her, in what she had discovered. If, with each new find, her very being seemed to sag, her avidity was undiminished. We had a kind of success and our several shows—individual and joint—were well-attended. But always the knowledge that this was merely an out-of-the-way village was there to qualify our euphoria.

I have mentioned my bitterness towards her, and my adoration, yet neither, as I think over what I've written, comes through, in my account. Let me say then that night after night, when finally I crept in beside her, her arms would open and draw me down and in that warmth I knew an ease so old it seemed I had never, in this existence, experienced. She was fit, too, for any kind of loving I was in the mood for. Whatever I began, she would finish, with equal vehemence. Loving, where the heart truly is moved, come times when it is impossible to know, where oneself ends, and the other begins. These times are rare I suspect because they are so hard to bear. I loved her simply and if that form of

39

happiness were all, I would have had enough. But loving her, I couldn't get enough of her, and our quarrels became notorious among the neighbors. But the allergy—or allergies—are maybe more to blame than any one other fact.

Sometimes I think hers came first. However that was, soon neither of us could put our hands in the hypo without a sudden numbness of the fingertips and, shortly thereafter, the entire finger—fingers, and soon, hands, and wrists, and limb. I have heard of immunities wearing off through too much exposure and the notion must have come from that. I've heard, too, that during the People's Park troubles in Berkeley, certain photographers, who had left their rolls of film containing evidence of police brutality, with local merchants, never got that film back. That must have given me the idea for what follows.

After we had contracted together this disease, we formed the habit of taking our film to an old man down the street, who kept a drugstore. It was the only one on the island and he was slow, and inept, but our one chance. He was fast sinking into decrepitude however and I first had this confirmed when he mislaid a roll of film, a series of self-portraits, I had taken him. I have never felt my own presence—physical, spiritual—in any shape or form— had that realness to it I find constantly in others. My rages, with their bellowings and bangings, are to be traced to this sense of being missing, I think. One is so almost overwhelmed even amid calmest circumstances. Pictures, therefore, are an enormous solace. Evidently one *had* been present, despite one's contrary impressions. Now the old man had lost the most recent such evidence and despair, absurdly, mounted. I shot another roll and in time those pictures came back—barely recognizable, so shoddy a job he'd done, but sufficient for the time being. I was calmer and enabled to give attention to my wife's latest work, those vacant landscapes she would patiently explain, dot by dot practically, were vivid with correspondence. The focus shifted alarmingly from picture to picture and often I would stare into them for minutes before I could grasp the scale. It was then I first began to fear the full extent of her sickness.

Yet it is the work of that period that currently enjoys such popularity. People I have never met, of altogether dubious validity,

40

stop me in the street to comment on them. They are tourists of course—the locals have a life apart from art, except as they're subjects for mine, and given that their daily round can be called *a life*—given, that is, there is someone to name it at all. After the old man died I could no longer pursue my calling and now spend my days doing whatever I please—little enough, I suspect, although since I find it so difficult to remember, I can't be sure. I have my collection and I know by looking at that, the time passes. Nobility, avidity, lust, indifference—what used to be called the whole range of human emotion, is registered here, if one will only look—though the expression often contradicts the accompanying feeling.

Here's hers, the print I wanted you to see . . . see the lateral series of shadows, narrowing to a finger, that twig, there, then, across the gap, as if reflected, almost a man's outstretched arm—that trapezoid—then, these rhomboids here. The record that light was placed in relation to, or "hovered," above, that plant? I think it a true photo, whatever—though all I have to go on is, the odor of hypo it triggers, so that with a rush every detail of my father's darkroom and person, wells up, and saves me from all else, so full the feeling is—in me. He was a bitter man.

The Boarders

This is only a story, all the more a ghost story for that fact, I think. Already I feel the relief of telling it—come in a cluster of time, to be hammered out, translucently or thinly opaque, in time. And when I reflect on what else I might be doing, I see just how much this is a ghost story.

But I'd best stop this insistence in case your disappointment— A friend, a woman, but more of an acquaintance, after all, I didn't know her very well, had invited me, or I suggested it, to spend the night with her, in this haunted house. Not to pass another night in the same old place—! I was very excited. I am now, my heart pounds, anxious not to leave anything out, that I might miss the opportunity. My parents taught me to be thrifty in my performances. And to mean what I say. Though what they meant, at every turn, by their instructions. . . . I want to give the details, let them speak for me, let it be their tale.

After we'd eaten dinner, I said to her, When? Any time now, she answered, I thought she was oddly off-hand. That's the thing—it's unpredictable, but you can count on it. Soon, if not now. She was a beautiful woman. That is, her face pleases me, even now, torments me, for of course she isn't, as I write this, present. Tormented me then, though, such pleasure it gave me in its openness, the veiled eyes, concealing so much from me, that I had to insist.

How shall we pass the time, until it begins? Silence was not possible to endure, besides, how could I manipulate it, so to speak, manage it, to make her like me more, so that she would reveal herself to me? We could tell each other stories, she smiled. But while I waited for her to, she wouldn't begin. So that I thought myself to be the first, but impatient, I suppose, deciding I wasn't about to speak, she switched on the radio. The music was continuous, that is, it was an FM station, with no or few interruptions to sell one something, and I went along with it, it took me along, slowing me down too, to keep its time, making a story of me with itself. I feel it right now, and then, recalling our purpose, I broke its spell, forcing myself, if only not to sit there all night, and nothing to show for it, next day.

Well—I began, but she spoke almost at once: I can't say why it hasn't started, so I saw that, suddenly, she was extremely nervous, she twisted the knob, flipping through several stations almost at once. She came to no decision, I thought, letting it stop in the course of a newscast—doubtless the sound of a voice had been what she wanted. She seemed calmer. But it was only the same old stuff, all I recall being some expert had forecast, whatever the race now did or did not do, it would in 35 more years erase itself. Listen, she said, Did you really *believe* that bullshit about ghosts? It was just something I made up, because I was so bored. Don't look so *disappointed,* I mean, I got you here.

I was still thinking of everything she could conceivably mean when she stood up abruptly, That stuff's getting to me, I've got to lie down, the bedroom's this way.

I don't get it, I said, sitting on its edge, What's to get? she grinned, Well, what's in it for you, you know I'm, I mean, I don't *need* an affair, or whatever, what is it, I mean in the morning, where will it be? I can't promise any continuity. Why *me?* You're an alluring woman, you could pick out anyone, why not someone who's lonely? She looked back at me, when I brought myself to turn around, with what I took to be hate. It passed, she smiled, Let's just say I figure it'll clear up my asthma. Her blouse was unbuttoned and when I leaned over her she reached a hand with a kind of detached vigor inside my shirt, ruffling it back and forth, that smooth hand, over the useless hair on my chest.

You knew all along, right? Did she actually say that? Coming, with all my concentration pacing the sensation, remembering to relax—it was almost perfect, so nearly what, suddenly, I'd wanted, but what about her—I'd remembered not to worry about her, but had those ambiguous grunts been her release, or hadn't she only just begun, wild movements that forced me on ahead of her, to climax? But lying back, my legs floating, I let go, as she sat up and lit a cigaret. I lied, she said. This place *is* haunted. But I wanted to fuck too. She went on talking, with more earnestness in her voice than I'd heard before, but I kept slipping in and out of sleep, until she got up, so I sat up, I'm hungry goddam it, she said, crossing the floor—her nakedness, it was like being blind, the form I had so desired, or desired sight of, bringing with it its own conditions of sight so it seemed however long and intensely I looked at her, the instant she was out the door and into the kitchen, I would forget, dim memories at best—and so it was. Fuck, she called, there *isn't* anything to eat. She reappeared, munching on a hunk of bread. Crumbs dropped onto the sheet. She had the transistor with her, now it was Mozart, I lay back to dig it, a reverie, such beauty, her elbow stuck me in the ribs, with her free hand she started to caress my belly, like sandpaper. Then it was midnight: The village had to be destroyed in order to save it, a genial voice reported. She began to talk, indistinctly, still eating. When I was in New York, dancing, I worked in this office, well, this man, an older man, kept coming in, well then his wife, once, there's this little winery, after work, waiting to hear from the agency, so that—so that after the final curtain the two of them, it was a very unusual apartment, and her breast brushed, or for some time had been resting against, my chest, that now filled my vision, Hmmm, she felt at me, Hmmm.

Why that, of all stories? Not right now, I thought—what was that? What happened, I persisted, but she wasn't listening, not to me. We relaxed, a siren. She handed me another drink.

But I couldn't, not all the way, let go. Things had their matter-of-fact presence, so I was at least that high, her thigh, of course, what else, but, how reasonable! but how wonderful, reason, her, a, woman, thigh! What, too, had happened, to the time? The TV was already on, some dawn "college of the air," a professor explicating, art, What happened, then? I asked, but then I was saying, almost in tears, Christ, where are those—just one, please, that's all, can't you conjure them, is it all a put-on? Someone was making sense of the news. And then we heard it: a sound, a step. But it was only the old couple, upstairs, in their apartment, getting up, she said—I bet we kept them awake all night, I think

44

they worry about me. You'd better get going, now. They make things tough, with the landlady.

I waited for her to invite me back, but even when I was out of the shower, and dressed, she hadn't spoken. Then, That's the breaks, she said, Sometimes they don't make it.

Rage took me over—it was her indifference, I explained, later. I'll be back tonight, I said. But at last she had become fully serious. You think I'm kidding, I'm not, but they destroy, do you know what you're doing? Then remember what I told you. Fuck that, I said, I don't care. I was determined to return. I'll take the place apart, upstairs too, board by board, to make them walk.

Color

They come in and tell their stories, he complained, I don't know what all the excitement's *about*. They get me all worked up but I've grasped nothing.

One had brought him an atlas, a street-guide to London, and he sat next to her, after their visitor had left, turning the pages with growing discomfort—I'm so foolish, I'm shaking, there's this movie I see, on every page, he said, I forget it's just lines on paper, to you. No, she said. I make up my own movies, because I want to be there, with you. Isn't that cozy, he laughed. Even if I took you there, where would it all be? Two movie-theaters moving hand-in-hand down Piccadilly. Telling one another stories to help the time pass, like Gretchen—and I hit on Mick, and I hit on Paul, and I hit on Jim, and what does it matter if she did or not, who's to know, what's *to* know, and didn't she go to all that trouble just for people like us, how is it real if she doesn't have friends who believe. But what does it matter, that we do, she was so spaced, how did she know what was there to be known.

Both of them sat silent, before the fire, which held their attentions, his, now hers, unfocused in the flickering. I'll tell you a story, she said then, but you'll have to copy it down, and we'll see what you heard, of what I said. It happened to a friend. Someone I knew before I knew you. You weren't always so important. Maybe my lover, maybe not, you'll never know. Then ask me. No, not like you, anyway.

While she was talking he had gone backstage at this girl's invitation. Her face had a vivacity that made its features hard to remember. She slipped her arm through his, strolling down the Avenue, towards the cast party. I thought you were fine, he told her, happy to be able to mean it. You brought such a candor to the role. She had kept on her stage make-up, for the party, and he thought perhaps this was the cause of the freedom he felt, speaking to her, stranger as she was; for this face was still that of the woman whose intimate life he'd been a party to, the past three hours. Yes, I think so too, she said agreeably. It was hard work. Identifying the gestures, you know, that would mean that, what did you call it? Candor. He liked her for not wasting their time with the customary self-deprecations.

They sat on the front steps, smoking. They had found themselves in agreement: the party was a drag. Shapes came up by them, towards it, the expressions difficult to decode in the shadow, presumably hopeful; one couple, their faces lit up when the front door opened, wore identically diffident masks, We're here, but not really. Don't put yourself out on our accounts. Just because it's your party.

He laughed, liking the way she had fixed them. People leaving were only shoulders, backs, legs, and they invented expressions for them, fitting phrases to them too. As each cluster left, the music from inside throbbed out to them. Where were you, when you first heard it, he said, meaning the music. My roommate, Patti, went to England, she sent a record. What a sad chick! Her father sent her everything she wore and, like, asked for it back, every time he wrote. Beautiful face, good body, too, but, those clothes. He laughed again, what wouldn't be amusing, bouncing the ball back, Let's take ours off, he said. Oh I don't know. Yes, it's cold, even though I've plugged in the heater there hasn't been time for the place to warm up, yet. The lights are out aren't they. Yes, there's just this red glow, and your body is red with it, but dimmer. So real, I can't believe it, kissing and sucking. I can't hardly bear it. Can you see our bodies he said, so that you'd know us, anywhere? Those legs that strutted, on stage. Didn't we kiss? Yes. In the taxi going home, too, before we got to this. You thought it was too corny, you broke up. I put that in because it's true, it's truer if it doesn't go too smoothly, like my coming before I wanted to, the first time. In the morning, in the daylight, talking on my phone, he said. Then I saw more of you, your beauty—turning shapes, I don't see too clearly, I stared too hard, at the time. Why didn't you come back—Don't ask me, she said, I don't want to tell. He said: You're a stranger. I hate you. I've always hated you. I despised you, to keep you alive. I was miserable, enabled to long for you.

That's a wonderful story? she said, putting out her smoke and rising. Thanks for telling me it. Thanks for letting me tell it, I never felt so much myself, as when I was in it. Was she about to go? No, she came up behind him, to look over his notes. How come there wasn't any make-up on the pillow, she asked. Because they had lain the wrong way round, he said.

THE ROLE OF INTELLECT
IN EVOLUTION

A Beautiful Woman

A beautiful woman enters the restaurant and immediately creates a sensation. Why is a woman as gorgeous as she is, as elegant, as radiant, as desirable, dining alone? As she is shown to a table, every head cranes to catch the sound of her voice, for she is about to speak to the waiter. Her voice, now she speaks, is revealed to be as thrilling and disturbing as her appearance and her carriage. "I am thirsty. Please bring me a glass of wine." Instantly, a hundred wine-glasses are extended towards her—each glass, the better to hold the vintage of her choosing, newly emptied.

One-Dimensional Dan

Dan needed a part-time job while going to college. He had gotten the address from the college newspaper, and when he got there, he looked around the room and got a sinking feeling in his stomach. He could identify either personally or through recognizing the type a number of go-getters from graduate school. The boss-to-be-if-one-got-lucky, who identified himself as Lucky, sat them down and told them to copy down a passage he then started to dictate. If Dan were to get this job, he would get nine dollars a lecture for copying down and typing up what some professor read to his class. Rumor had it that some professors read to their class from identical sets of notes such note-takers had typed up in previous years, putting in just enough changes to keep the process going. Lucky started to dictate. Dan started to copy it down. Then he stopped. He had identified the passage. When they were all sent home to type up their notes, he got the book out and started in copying out the passage, stopping now and then to insert errors in order not to appear implausibly perfect. Then he got on his bike and after a passage of time he got off. He started down a passage and stopped by the office to insert his copy in the boss-to-be's box.

After a brief passage of days Dan was sent for. Lucky got straight to the point. He said he himself had inserted errors and these Dan had not copied down since he had stopped copying as soon as he had identified the passage. No point, Dan saw, in professing outrage at this deception. He got up to go. Stop, Lucky said. Sit down. I like it, he said, that you were able to identify a passage from *One-Dimensional Man.* You can start tomorrow. Dan had gotten lucky. And Lucky had gotten Dan. I got the job! Dan told his wife. And two weeks later he was still saying this to her. Only he was inserting the word *lousy* between the article and its noun.

Society's Child

When two of Brian's colleagues, Kate and Helen, dropped by unannounced one morning and told Brian's wife Vera that they were taking him to a conference, she betrayed her usual lack of surprise and sent him off with a kiss and a casual "See you tomorrow."

Brian didn't recall having expressed interest in this conference, but he enjoyed the company of Kate and Helen, whom he regarded as two of the boys, and welcomed the relief from writing his dissertation. And he was one of those who welcome the unexpected. He even went looking for it, you might say, despite the contradiction implicit therein. And he liked long drives in cars, the new scenery, the sensuous continuous motion.

He hadn't any money, so he would somehow have to smuggle himself into the conference. And he couldn't pay for a room, but Kate and Helen said that he could stay in theirs. That was piquant as a notion, Brian thought. Maybe they wanted him to watch. He had a rule against thinking anything through to the end, he enjoyed the under-defined. *Que sera, sera.* If it was good enough for Doris Day and all those European soccer fans, it was good enough for him.

It was a large, old hotel, there among the sheltering palms of the Peninsula. Brian recalled a song by his friend Ray Rockaway, "Down in Palo Alto/ Where the palmtrees touch the sky/ A thousand Pee Aitch Dees/ Are asking 'Why?' " He sang it to Kate and Helen as they walked through the lobby.

"Next year, it'll be a thousand and three," Helen reminded him.

"I have my doubts about thee and me," he replied. "Kate may make it. She has a containable topic. You and me are all over the place." Yes, Kate was sitting pretty—"Changing Modes of

54

Reference to the Male Sexual Organ" . . . Brian couldn't call to mind the historical and geographical limits she'd set herself. Maybe she'd like to refer to mine, he thought. He'd never really thought of showing it to Kate. She didn't go in for glamor in a big way. She had no come-on. But here, in their room, which had large twin beds, as the three washed up after their long drive, the unaccustomed intimacy was opening his eyes—or closing them. He remarked, not for the first time, the parasexual affections so readily demonstrated between women, an ease in touching, in the offer to lend a blouse. Aware of them moving about the room in this ritual of preparation, he felt the two were one, readying themselves to present to a group the image of woman. Each made disarming confessions to the other about so-thought flaws of appearance, in the act of disguising these flaws. Connubial, he thought. Of course he couldn't tell how much of this was because he was present. Attention was certainly being drawn to their bodies. Vera was convinced that Kate and Helen were lesbians, probably lovers; because his wife was usually proven right, sooner or later, in her decisions about the people they knew, Brian had accepted this diagnosis—until now.

Helen—Kate being in the bathroom—was asking him to help her hook her bra. So there were her naked back and sides, the glimpse of a breast that made his hand suddenly tingle and ache, and juice appear in his mouth. He allowed she might derive pleasure from taunting him with the prohibited made visible. But he couldn't be sure. Which she could count on. Her manner wasn't settled. A sisterly disregard of his sight of her skin could not suppress a wicked sidewise glint. He started to say "Helen, what do you have in mind?" But Kate came back out just as he said her friend's name. Helen said "Yes?" Brian replied "Oh, nothing. I only wondered which panel you were going to go to first."

Turned out to be one both he and Kate figured would be of interest too. And from there they went to the dinner. And after dinner, they moved to the bar, in company with Dr. Whitesides, the renowned scholar. So that Brian was never alone with either Helen or Kate after that minute in their room. Not that he would have put to Kate the question he'd nearly put to Helen. About Kate was a gruffness he wouldn't penetrate. But both women were at their most charming now. Irving Whitesides was a catch. Brian couldn't recall what it was this pompous elderly bore was famous for, but he was sure it couldn't be spontaneous *conversazione*. A loneliness welled out of the man, although he was not what his manner suggested, a solitary bachelor, for he spoke of his wife and teenage children on several occasions. He was quite proper, but the attentions he paid to Helen she clearly found flattering. Her pale blue eyes sparkled. She accepted another brandy. The younger man wrestled with his dislike of the older, pointing out to himself the obvious. Yet there it was. Anytime, he told himself, anywhere, this man would be objectionable.

Kate was also animated, and in her excitement, let her thigh press against Brian's, there on the banquette. Testing, he shifted away. She followed. Leveling with himself, Brian had to admit he wanted neither woman, it was the situation he found intriguing, that lent a glamor to them that, alone, he doubted he would find. He definitely didn't mean to end up with Kate while Helen went off with Whitesides. If *that* was their little game. If there *was* any game. He was getting drunk. He remembered the moment when the three of them had left their room, the women giggling to one another, moving ahead while he locked the door. Legs, rumps, stockings and high heels, ahead, along the corridor, showing him the way. He was drawing a line around the unknown, to make himself hot for it. He did this for love of such heat.

Dr. Whitesides beamed distantly upon them all. It was high time they retired, tomorrow would be a busy and exacting day, but he hoped the three of them would do him the honor of being his guests at dinner when the conference was ended. This would mean getting home very late but none of them wished to worry about that now. So they accepted. As they rode up together in the elevator Whitesides asked the women what floor they were on. They told him. He turned to Brian. Helen's face suddenly glowed with mischief. "And you?" Brian was preparing to say that his own room was on the same floor as theirs, but his own drunkenness and the mechanical nature of Whitesides' questions, as predictable as everything he had said all evening, made him giggle. It was only a brief lapse, he recovered and started to speak his piece, but he had set Helen and Kate off, they were reeling helplessly against the elevator walls. It reminded Brian of the way everybody laughed after Lights out in scout camp, hysterically, set off by the merest syllable. Whitesides watched them, coldly puzzled. Helen began to explain. They felt—or so Brian felt— the older man's misunderstanding of their relationship, which was, Brian saw in a flash, quite innocent.

But the good doctor had heard their giggles.

"Let me," he said, when they had at last gained some self-control, "Let me, young man, offer you the spare bed in my room. That strikes me as much more, um, proper. Unless, that is . . . ?"

To take him up on that "unless" was not possible, Brian realized. Careers were at stake. Grumpily, he accepted.

In the man's room, Brian surrendered, let the drinks take over, hardly spoke with his new roommate at all but, collapsing into the spare bed, went straight to sleep.

Waking, the room, empty, already filled with daylight, he recalled an arrangement, that all four of them should meet for breakfast in the hotel coffee-shop. He hurried downstairs but didn't find Helen or Kate until nearly noon, leaving a panel. They said Whitesides hadn't shown up for breakfast either—but when they'd run into him at the first panel, he'd been distant and said nothing about their dinner date. His strangulated speech, his averted gaze—hungover? Had he been drunker than they'd realized, the night before?—the women had found confusing, wounding. Could Brian throw any light on this change in his behavior? Brian could not. He told them how he had fallen instantly asleep. "After you turned me in," he nearly added. But Whitesides wasn't the only one to act more distant, today—"The morning after," Brian thought. Then added, again to himself: "After a big nothing." Maybe they all were feeling something of that. Maybe not. If Vera was right, Kate and Helen had had one another. To his companions, he responded flippantly, comparing Dr. Whitesides to the millionaire in "City Lights." "You will recall," he said, not doing either of them the discourtesy of supposing she would not have seen the film, "that when drunk, he either wanted to fling himself into the river—and I found the old boy to exude a suicidal moroseness—or to party with Charlie. But once he was sober, he was a real stuffed shirt and wouldn't even recognize him."

Kate and Helen found no satisfaction in such slight wit of analogy. They had, far more than he, the scholar's impulse, to dig and keep digging, and they had a fund of negative energy that made them think they were digging for the dirt. Brian's butterfly mind missed yesterday's hysteria. His eyes closed and he slid sideways in the back seat, which he had to himself on the drive back. Hazily, then more distinctly, he believed he heard his mother and his older sister speaking, arguing in a cozy way, perhaps about his father. In his trance, he assigned Kate to his sister, Helen to his mother—and then hazily studied the inconsistencies, Kate's gruffness reminding him more of his, *their*, he had thought, mother, Helen's lovely blue eyes calling to mind his voluptuous sister. . . . How cozy to lie dozing, lapped in their presences, watched over in this way!

When Brian woke, they were only a few miles from his home. Now *he* felt hungover, a delayed reaction, tongue dry and head throbbing. What had he dreamed? Whitesides scolding him, standing over him, virtually shouting. "You're sick. You need psychiatric help. You're sick." The tone was that of his father, ordering him to get up, because he was late for school. The dream was curiously real, curiously elusive. The incident had occurred minutes after Brian had fallen asleep in the older man's room. Obviously Whitesides had been outraged at the bizarre bedroom arrangements of his young colleagues, and, unable to contain himself, had shouted Brian into wakefulness in order to counsel him. In my dream, Brian added quickly, realizing he was treating this image as though it belonged to the waking order of reality. Which of course, it didn't. In fact, even as he watched the mental image, it began to shift, and he saw that Whitesides was raging at Brian because Brian had rejected his advances: naked from the waist down, the famous scholar was shouting up at Brian from the floor next to the bed, where Brian had shoved him. "You're sick! Cunt-struck! Too sick for real love!" Brian couldn't help noticing the tiny, shriveled penis. But this had not so much the feeling-tone of a dream as the meretricious feel of a masking image.

But now Helen, noticing he was sitting up, sang out with renewed cheer (or a fair simulation of cheerfulness): "It's almost time to say bye-bye, darling! Too bad we couldn't spend the night together! I wonder if we'll ever have another chance. . . ."

"I'm sure we will," he answered with the required amount of insincerity in his voice, while mindful also of dramatic irony. But in truth he was only going through the motions to mask from the others his growing distraction. For now with that inward eye that is the bliss of solitude, he saw himself blundering drunkenly over to Whitesides' bed and yanking the covers back, beginning to run his hands over the body thus exposed—made randy, Brian thought with pathetic self-exoneration, by the frustration of a long day's titillation. And then he saw the picture change again. . . . Whitesides was reprimanding him *after* they had finished with one another. He was accusing Brian, then, of leading *him,* the older man, astray. . . . But now the car was stopping in front of his house. Giving first Kate then Helen a brief kiss on the lips, he started up the stairs to his house.

"See you in the library!"

"If I don't see you first! Love ya!"

Vera gave him a big hug. "Have fun?"

"The usual rollicking good time one has at scholarly sessions. Don't stop hugging."

"Where did you stay?"

"With the extinguished scholar Irving Whitesides."

"Does he snore?"

"In Hittite. Anything to eat?"

God, he was glad of Vera. The dream he'd had in the back seat of the car—for of course, it had been just a dream, Brian realized—had left him feeling vulnerable, even powerless. Thank God he'd had the good sense to marry Vera! What a good wife. . . . And now he had best go straight to his study and get on with that dissertation. There had to be a way to cut it down to size. He had wasted altogether too much time already.

David's Rod

So there among the archetypes we find the boy-child in the at least emotional absence of whose father the mother turns to and finds in his loneliness a ready response until the pair of them are hopelessly entangled till death takes not one but both and the pain of her intrusion finally is numbed.

Now, age 33, he took his bandages in his hands and leaned up. He gave his wife/mommy a boy-child, thanked her for the ride, which was in fact not far, just up the hill to the undocumented apartment she had picked for him off the Co-op bulletin board, and settled in to deal with the first fact of his new life, a huge red cock which had escaped. Grievously remiss as his character had proven to be, so what? He put the blame where it belonged. "When a woman has got children, she thinks the world wags only for them and her. Nothing else. The whole world wags for the sake of the children—and their sacred mother." "That's damned true," he told himself. And the strange, piercing keenness of daybreak's sharp breath was on him.

People had taken to the streets. Police had dragged them off to jail. The number of students applying to the psychiatric ward for help had dropped drastically. All hell was breaking loose— aye, and heaven too. "Move in with me—can't you tell true love when you hold it in your arms, when your cock is fusing you with it?" Were her eyes too bulbous, her skin-tones a shade too sallow, as he bowed and took leave of the archetype she'd performed for him? But there was the boy, too. Two weeks later she was engaged to a guy who looked a lot like himself. As for himself, there was someone he needed to meet, who also looked a lot like himself. If it doesn't get done sooner, it has to get done later, and bad luck for those in the way. They should think of themselves as messengers, helpers, goddesses and daemons. But they should think of themselves.

He would see the boy twice a week. He would no longer live with the woman who had suddenly turned to him and said: Why don't you stop messing around with poetry and pass your Latin exam? Of course, she had provocation. He would stop messing about with poetry, and get down to it. And he would pass his Latin exam. He would miss her income, also. But be damned and blasted to women and all their importances. They want to get you under, and children is their chief weapon. And the cock, with the flat, brilliant glance, glanced back at him, with a bird's half-seeing look. Crowing triumph and assertion, yet strangled by a cord of circumstance. His voice ran on easily and garrulously, carefully dressing panic. How terrible that it should be spring, warm with hot, brooding female bodies, on the brink of fainting in all the anguish of their generation's forlornness! And that there is the soul, begging definition.

He shut the book, locked the door, walked towards the campus. At the edges of rocks, he saw the silky, silvery-haired buds of the scarlet anemone bending downwards. And why not, he thought to himself, why not. These things around him were in a world that had never died. There are records. An elderly woman in a Bentley, believing herself unseen, hunted boogers. Perfumes were coming from his body as if from some strange flower. The present lay below, already burning, a pathetic corkscrew with a huge reverberating wine. He thought of all he might do: drive to visits (but he no longer had wheels), walk in the opposite direction (but this he was already doing), or go through the little iron gate, be startled by the rippling, flapping overlapping of soft bells (the windchime).

Rare women wait for the re-born man. Was this woman in the record store not one of them? The door stood open. The all-tolerant Pan watched over them. They should be so lucky. They sat together in her all-tolerant pad, watching her four-year-old play with his toy snake. He was chopping it into tiny, tiny pieces. And she must find his hands and his feet, his heart, his thighs (be still, Woody Allen), his head, his belly, and fold her arms round the re-assembled till it became warm again, and could embrace her.

Her face was rather long and pale, her dusky red hair held under a thin gold net. Men had tortured her half to death with their touch. Well done. You made it! she reassured him as he lay panting and spent beside her rather long, pale form on the mattress on the floor. The long-sloping fall of haunches from the socket of the back sobbed bitterly. It was all part of the general catastrophe, another feather floating in the chasm, if people are wisps of smoke. Malls were already more than a thought on a drawing-board. Now he had tried one of her, and, worse, she, one of him. Soon the bears would be back for the reckoning. In Baden-Baden, he recalled, in 1528, a regulation had ordained that if a man forsake his wife and children, said wife and children were at once to be sent after him, and would arrive the next day, like forwarded mail. It took longer these days. Thus ended the first week for the man who cut his hair and his beard after the right fashion, and smiled to himself.

If, then, the object perceived is self, what is the subject that perceives? The library, he thought, being where he sat. Or if it is the true self which thinks, what other self can it be that sinks its sins in syntax? Very well, poetry. A secret self I had enclosed within, that was not bounded by my clothes or skin. "It's just love," she said cheerfully. Would she say anything cheerfully? Some women wear skirts to make men get on with it. Slowly he climbed the denuded knoll, faint and rosy, the rosiness the outpouring of white-hot solitude. The infuriating dome. The only one that exists. In contradistinction to what is adventitious. "The better the life he lived, the higher they raised him from the waters." Libra, watch that tendency to equivocate! All tough rubber goods bore a sense of foreboding. His tiny apartment, wedged into the hillside, didn't officially exist. An object passed his Latin exam, one with his name driven into it, and on the other hand, the English crib write small from wrist to fingertip. If that was the adult world, ave atque vale. A wedge of his brain had been removed while he slept by educated hands. He needed his radio, that worked if propped up at one end with a copy of *Aaron's Rod.* The dial was stuck on KYA. "You say you seen seven wonders/ and your bird is green/ but you don't see me. . . ." Easy for them to sing that.

A cage or cave of its kind, giving onto the flatlands, densely peopled, and the Bay beyond, studded with tankers. On a clear day, the spires and turrets conglomerate of SF. Rusk spoke and blood streaked the walls. Time gets rolled up in voices. But at some point a particularly remarkable molecule was formed by accident, precocious concept. "Hey, it's me!" It's all here. Examine your own sperm. It's a mosaic. Yet, you did it. Were there when it happened. Release of loneliness, bitter burden—felt in shoulders, neck: as if literal, a person sitting there, to be borne across some hard-to-imagine Bosporus. Sadness: that you can't live another's life for them, they you neither. Have a drink. Never, alone. As if it could be known.

Takes body for healthy walk, here and there, tufts of harebells blue as bubbles. I am that I am from the sun, brilliant here this morning, and others are not my measure. Inconceivable arrogance, not to say blindness, mouthful of words his father must have spat out. He went on, along the streets and walkways laid out for, if not him, some person deceptively like him. Likewise the campus, crammed with books and persons to read same. "Spare change?" She was pleased with the money, and now she wanted to take more from him. "Smile?" But he would not be touching the little, personal body, and so he told her: "My mother was just hit by a truck." His grant had been renewed. The day of their interfering with him was done, he told himself, for another six months. Somewhere afar, borne faintly on the breeze, a rooster did some subtext. Weary of walking, he turned into a cafe and stopped at the first table.

There sat Sue-Ellen Maymont, her blue blazer and gray slacks out-of-place among the Bohemians of the Cafe Med. She was slumming. But for him she had the dazzling smile. He was about to find out that she had just started The Pill and had come seeking the man of her choosing.

At this time, in the USA, 52% of the population were female, a high proportion of them young. Statistics also support the thesis that more of the 48% than the 52% were homosexual. That date with himself was going to have to wait. And from the pebble of bliss, the ripples of misery spread to the edge of the Berkeley human loch.

The prophet had cast the first stone. His mother had told him not to.

Some of these phrases come from various works of David Herbert Lawrence, among these *Aaron's Rod* and *The Man Who Died.*

The Role of Intellect in Evolution

The boy was crying as if his heart would break. He was four years old. His mother had had to go away for two days and Brian was there to take care of him. The boy's crying was starting to get to him. Brian could hardly tell anymore where it was coming from, inside or outside. Kids were definitely uncool. You couldn't very well ask them to smoke a joint and space out, although he once had been present when some friends of friends, having blown smoke into a Co-op bag containing the cat, which then had emerged to stretch itself out purring on a cushion, turned their attention to their baby, speculating that its fretfulness perhaps could be eased by exhaling in its direction. Brian had left about then. He wasn't very cool himself, he realized. Things quickly got too oceanic for his liking. Upright, uptight, in the white sense. He leaned heavily on analysis, he thought. Now, he told himself, he should figure out the problem then come up with a solution. He would do this by talking to the boy. Then he would figure out what was best to tell him.

He called to mind all he knew of the boy's history. Somewhere in there must lie the clue to this terrible tantrum. Once we find the cause to any effect, we're at least halfway to replacing the effect we don't like with one that we do. Well, Brian knew that the boy's father had left when he was only two, and that this had no doubt made the boy uncommonly insecure about a parent's absence. The best thing to tell him would be the truth, that his mother though obviously absent tonight would only be gone for one more day and one more night. You know how long a day is, he went on, raising his voice to be heard as the howls grew louder. I mean, how short. You know, how not long. And how not long a night, right? Well, just add one not-long day to one not-long night. That's not very long at all, really, is it?

The boy began to shriek. Brian had been about to break a day down into component parts, breakfast, going for a walk, lunch, having a friend over to play, dinner, tv, teeth-brushing, bedtime story, sleep, but under the assault of the child he not only couldn't be heard, he couldn't think straight. Completely at a loss, he took the boy in his arms and said, I know, you miss your Mommy. All he could do was repeat this, rocking the slight body as he did so. He felt the rigidity go out of it. The crying quietened. I know, you miss Mommy. The boy let himself be held, sobbing only once in a while, until Brian realized he had gone to sleep.

A Use of Art

for M.
"I also ate at that arcade"

A man went into a Berkeley bookstore one day in 1966 shortly after the break-up of his marriage and was told by the woman behind the counter to read the *Memories, Dreams and Reflections* of Carl Jung. Hold the ladder steady while I mount it and I'll get you what you need, she told him. As she came down, flushed with her exertion, she smiled easily and said, I get a rash if I wear panties. I hope you enjoy it as much as I do, and she handed him the book. Why don't I come over around midnight tonight and we'll talk over what you've been able to look at so far. You don't know where I live, he stammered. Isn't this your address? she handed him a slip of paper. Yes, he said, How did that get there? You wrote it down while I was up the ladder, she replied. But you don't even know my name, he persisted. She told him what his name was, adding, Oh, I know your *name* all right. Her smile was radiant, beyond the shadow of a doubt. You're Libra, cusp of Scorpio, Introverted, Intuitive, which is how you know *my* name is Helen. See you later.

And it was considerably later than midnight before she arrived. He could have sworn he'd locked his door but there she was, already in the room with him. Helen, he'd been musing, hadn't his friend Sapir mentioned he was having an affair with a Helen who worked in a bookstore? But he had no time for further reflection. How on earth did you get in here, are you a phenomenon of solitude, he cried. A psychic compensation, an hallucination? But the synchronistic fingers had him by the balls.

Daniel and Helen met in this manner several times more, and

67

he discovered more concerning her prophetic powers. There was the night she read his Tarot and assured him of imminent sexual disappointment. There was the time she prophesied that, if he were only to consult his pubic hair, he'd find he had crabs. And so it was. Then one day, when they hadn't met for a while, she called to say she'd be at his place that midnight. What *did* she do all evening? I believe you're ready to be admitted to the next spiral of apprehension, she said down the wire, and in a blinding flash he was. Sapir is very, very fond of you, Daniel, Helen concluded. And you are not a petty person. I am not a petty person, Daniel found himself muttering as, at half past midnight, he put on his coat, turned out his light, locked his door and strode out into the darkened street. Not petty, he was still muttering as the car with the man and woman in it sped past in the direction of his place. There was so little light they could only have seen a man, walking. He knew his friend Sapir, though Greek, was naturalized, yet somehow had never registered with the draft-board. I will stop now, Daniel thought, I will turn him into the draft-board, then I myself shall join the USAF, he will be sent to Vietnam and so shall I, and one day I shall strafe his unit. Suddenly he was impatient to go home and write, otherwise his fantasy, which was growing thick and fast, would overwhelm him. Besides, the draft-board had been blown up the day before.

He could smell Helen's perfume, *Nuit de Stay-dee,* as he let himself in, but there was no note. There was no one to interrupt him and so he sat himself down and wrote the story of the war in Southeast Asia, he wrote the story of War, he wrote the story of the Return of the Repressed, of the Homosexual Element in Jealousy, he wrote the account of the Sexual Objectification of Woman, he wrote Finis to the Philosophy of Godlike Survey.

Years later, when he read in Santa Barbara, a woman came up to him at the party afterwards and objected to this poem. But in bringing these shadowy wishes and drives into the light, he urged gently, we don't advocate them, we interfere with their being acted out. I admit I had these impulses, but in such a way that I gained the control of them a poem can be. But you don't expect my husband to understand that, do you? When he gets me home tonight, he's going to make me get down on my hands and knees so he can check out my scar-tissue. Look at him, she hissed, indicating a pleasant-looking man murmuring to himself in a corner, I know him, right now he's imagining he's a B-52. Oh, I can't stand the sight of him! Let's go talk somewhere else— there's a stairway down the cliff. I can find my way down there blindfold.

In a Nutshell

Things hadn't been going too well lately, what with food-prices and the cost of gasoline and all, and the kids wanting to go to college and the missus having that meeting over to the house about the ERA, and then the cars having to go into the shop, one right after the other bam-bam like that, so it really did me good to see him smiling like he did, made me feel kinda warm inside, and I asked him, just like that, straight up and asked him how he did it, how come he could keep feeling so good the times being what they were. You know what he said? "Friend," he says to me, "you want to know what keeps me feeling so fine? I'll tell you what makes me feel so fine, so full of goodwill unto men and women, and I want you to listen up real careful, because I don't want you to miss anything. The reason I feel this good is because I believe in America and I believe in Tomorrow. That's it in a nutshell."

So I gave him all my money.

The Close of *Une Semaine de Bonté*
by Max Ernst

for R.G., again.

1

Upon a silver screen, these words were flashed: "You are in a room with a fish tank containing a pair of ragged hands and a light bulb yet curiously the room stays dark (the tank is backlit). This is because that light bulb is actually zillions of miles off— effectively beyond the control of anyone. In fact it's only been drawn in there, with its pathetic resemblance to a human face, to account for the hands in the tank. The hype is that they're under the control of that godlike-looking head. Now we have embodied this lesson for you, we will let you see the hands slither up out of the tank." With the accustomed alacrity of habit, they drain the water, spring the hinges and fold the tank up flat. The face on the light-bulb head remembers to smile. It takes on a resemblance to the Bhagwash of Hogwash, Oregon, and then it starts to look like your penis. Your penis is smiling at your hands— leering at them, like someone who sat through "The Mousetrap" forty times at the beginning of the denouement.

2

It was hot at the beach and David and Frieda Hand wore their darkest shades. They spread out their rattan roll-up mats and lay down on their tummies to catch some rays. How good to get out of Winnipeg for the winter! They kissed, lightly, touching lips like touching fingertips—a batlike squeak of a bit-of-alright, tin-tinnabulating like Swiss mountainmen loosening up on their alpenhorns. But the arms of the Law are longer and pretty soon its shadow falls across the pinkening forms of our erstwhile blissed-out couple. "A few questions, Darrell Tanner and Francie McCulloch, okay? It's about embezzlement, eh?" But even in their prison cells, Sol reached them, traversing space that is not space in time that is probably not time, either, leastways the way we tend to think of time. This isn't the kind of time you can do. And as each in his or her lonely cell recalls Honolu', a phantom of the other's self appears . . . ah so near, as a bird to the lime-twig! but the fingers are not, actually, touching, are they, and the darkness surrounds us, possibly the darker for the quality of the xerox.

3

The moon flooded the night, bouncing off a few puffy clouds about two-thirds of the way down the page on the right, and causing the two unclad bodies stilled by its magic on their blanket to blaze with reflected glory. A soft luminescence caused the forward, breaking waves to stand out. The lovers—the two soothing hands of the universe—prepared to commence their stroking, smoothing and fondling operations. "Isn't the moon a great idea, Bik?" one murmured. "I don't know about that, but he sure LOOKS like he's HAVING one right now, Vik. Don't you feel like you're in a work of art?" "How would that feel, Bik?" "Oh, sort of eternal and exciting and ambivalent all at the same time," replied Bik, wondering where he'd left the carkeys. Of that particular scene on that particular night, nothing remains—they were swept away. But we still have this scrap of paper. When we are old and bald and can no longer hang a false beard on our faces properly, and we are, and we can't, we will still be scrapping on paper. Your body is as mysterious as night and as nebulous as moonshine. But at least now your right hand knows what your left hand is doing. The rest is geometry. Aren't you glad you stopped biting your nails? The screen blanked out and we ate blancmange, wobbling in time with our mouths.

How to Write for a Reading

Terence Dactyl
Laurel at Bay
Phenobarbidol
California

Dear Professor Quatrain:

        I am the author of more than 17 (but probably no more than 18) volumes of poetry and prose (*Sickness Unto Death & Other Yarns, The Worm in the Bud Is My Buddy*), have published in a wide range (*Lonely Megaphone, Fichte Review*) of journals and magazines, and have given readings from my own works at college campuses all over the country. How are you? Your name was passed along by Anthony Anapest, who speaks of you with considerable warmth. And of course your article on the use of the syzygy in Bosnian folk-poetry is well-known to me, and Volume 83 of *The Comparative Pedant* is beside me as I write, open to pages 16–92. Keep up the good work!

        You may well wonder that I, a total stranger, should write to you. What could he possibly want of me, you are probably asking yourself at this very moment. Well, let me put you out of your misery! It just so happens that I'm to be in your neighborhood between either March 6–8, March 17–23, or September 11–12, on urgent business, and would be willing while there to make your acquaintance and to read on your campus. I customarily do this for a large sum of money but seeing that I'm going to be there anyway I will consider a pittance many would deem humiliating. It's not as though I'm not used to it, after all. This society treats its artists shamefully. It has to defend its clichés against the real news.

I'm well aware there are stories going the rounds about how I actually loathe giving readings, how I hate meeting professors and students, how flying gives me claustrophobia and airports, agoraphobia, and that I have a speech impediment and that this would prevent anyone understanding my poems even if they were written to be read aloud. So what. Him who striveth unceasingly upward, him alone can we save. It's unthinkable that you should invite Anapest and not invite me! Dr. Quatrain, I urge you to think long and hard about this matter. No one wants to be the laughing-stock of posterity, does he? I've read at a lot better places than Milltown State. More than 17, certainly.

Let me assure you there's no trace of ego left in me. Not I, but the wind that blows through me: what I stand for must be served. Every day men die miserably for want of the news. In this respect, I urge you to get my name right on the publicity. Last time I read, a considerable crowd showed up, hoping to hear *Crocodile* Dactyl. Latecomers kept interrupting to ask when I was going to play my Bushman's Mouth-harp. As they ought to have known, I perform unaided—the work requires no props. Unless, that is, a college wishes to pay the expenses of my friend Dexter, who juggles Indian clubs during my haiku sequence. But I'm not at all sure I want to read that sequence again. I'm not even sure that I haven't lost it. Let me just shuffle through these papers one more time. . . . Ah, here it is. . . . No, I don't believe I'll read this. . . . Or maybe I will. Tell you what, I'll wait and see how the mood takes me.

Tell you what, when I get there, you can help me decide. Need I say how much I look forward to talking with you? And with your good lady, who will get to meet a real poet at last? I only wish I could be there longer. I could stay long enough to conduct a workshop next day for the additional $50. I could stay overnight with you. I hear you've got a great place. Wonderful what one can do with a little tenure, isn't it? Funny thing, though—I don't suppose Shakespeare or Dante had tenure. But then, they didn't know a hell of a lot about Bosnian folk-poetry either.

So, we'll have plenty to talk about. If you think, though, that poets are too creepy to have around the house—understandably, after what Anapest did to your wife's and your front door—I can always sleep on the floor in your graduate assistant's loft beside the El in my neckbrace down in the industrial district.

I'll enclose a pamphlet of my latest poems. You'll notice that they read down as well as across. Watch out for the staples. If I don't read at Milltown, I want this back.

In concluding, I wish you all the best in your exacting profession. Wisdom goes hand in hand with age, and I hear you are quite old. I know you will want to see justice done before you die. For God's sake, Quatrain! All I want is what you paid Anapest—it can't have been as much as he says. But perhaps you are already dead. If so, please have the common courtesy to pass this along to the Committee on Visiting Writers. To whom I would like to say, sincerely, that I know what fine work each of you has been doing in recent years. Everything I said to Quatrain goes double for you. I realize you're probably junior faculty who regard this as one more duty dumped upon you because you can't say no until you get tenure. Look, why not simply give the entire semester's allotment to me? Look at the trouble you'll be saved. But of course you'll probably want to give it all to a "name" like Theodore Thoroughgood or Paul Skald or Bobby Bounty, who'll do the same old gig they always do—after all, that's what the rubes want, right? But perhaps you have the intellectual honesty to resist the easy way out.

However, if this letter turns up at the bottom of a stack of departmental memos two years from now, I know I will live as a guilty start in your heart.

Truly yours,
Terence Dactyl, Poet.

And Echo Answers Something

Professor Nixon sent me. He said only you can tell me if these poems are any good. I was going to kill myself when I woke up this morning, but then I decided to go to the city and find a publisher and get these published. But I want to verify first that they're worth doing that with. Because otherwise I would have a wasted trip to the city when I might be killing myself in my shack or I could do it right here on your rug. This is the best of them, of course I write in a number of selves but this is the closest to the self I choose to assume today. Of course it's all Reichian character armor, but I suppose you require me to dangle some kind of scarecrow before you. In my opinion it's the best we've had since Blake, but then I haven't read any other poets. Who needs them. Words are poor instruments. TM has shown me that. I don't know why I condescend to use them. It's just that I have this terrific talent—more of a sacred gift. If I can rescue others from the tyranny of words, it's my duty. I sent this one to the *New Yorker*. It's probably a bit askew to your alpha-waves. Don't ask me what it means. I compose spontaneously. I don't interpret. As Blake said, we murder to dissect. This is a pretty sharp-looking letter-opener. I never mention my father in any of my poems. I'm going to stop taking drugs. You don't know what they're cut with. I was sitting in my shack when I had a vision. It was a woman all in white. Her name was Hegel. Hegel—the greatest human being who ever lived, to whose memory I mean to dedicate all my efforts. I mean to reconcile Siddharta with Breughel, Lenin with Van Gogh, Einstein with Dante. Yes, man, I do a lot of reading. It's all shit—a bunch of words. I killed that veil of illusion and buried it. It's all imagery. No, I didn't need to actually read Hegel. She came in a vision and told me all I needed to know. She told me I have psychic powers. But no, I don't think for a minute I can transform the world without lowering myself to words. I mean pigs might fly. It's a long way down from this window—is that a parking lot? What are those things— those cows? Cars? I was going to drive to the city but I came straight here instead. It must mean something. Did you have a funny feeling before you saw me today? A premonition? Death has been on my mind lately. What else is there, really? This girl told me she liked my smile—the one I'm smiling now. Then she hurt herself, somehow. Fell backwards. What do you think? I want to know if you think it's publishable, that's all. Is that so much to ask? Of course, I know how busy you must be, seeing how much money the state pays you. You'd have to work real hard to be worth all that much. But I'm not asking for a lot of your time. You don't have to understand it—it's just a bunch of words that came to me when I was in the spaceship. That was on army maneuvers in Nam. They looked a lot like us. The company commander was Fred—he looked a lot like you. He was frozen to the spot. What? Stuck with the rules? Oh, a stickler. We were stuck with him. He got fragged. He was like a father to me. This paperweight—you could do a lot of damage with one of these. I mean, if your hand slipped while your arm was in the air. So, what do you think? Tell me frankly. It's a load of crapola, isn't it? No? You really think so? It's really very good? You say they'd be crazy not to publish it? I can't tell you how relieved that makes me. I'm tired of being rejected. Why, only last week I went to the State Hospital and tried to get myself admitted. They kicked me out."

"They kicked you out?"

"I told them I was crazy, but they wouldn't listen."

"Well—who are they to judge?"

Of a Night at the Master's

As you all know," our Master was saying, as I entered the room, a little out of breath from trying to find a parking place, "when young, I traveled extensively throughout America." This was the first time he had mentioned this, and I for one had a hard time believing it. But what he had to tell us turned a small doubt into its opposite.

"When I was barely 21 years old, at an age, that is, when, had I been the child of an American millionaire, I should have been disporting myself at some more or less fashionable university, learning what was then considered appropriate—French, Cubist Greek, or Homeric Expressionism, or Viennese prose-poetry, or How to Run a Bank—some subject, anyway, that would qualify me as *intelligent* on tests designed by professors of esthetics, economics, or the classics—I found myself, between jobs, passing, for the first time in my life, through Detroit.

"The job I was leaving, psychiatric aide in a mental hospital (we changed bedsheets) had paid $180 a month: today, that would be about $880, and I had most of my final check still on my person, so I was in no immediate danger of arrest for vagrancy.

"However, as is often the case in this unsteady post-industrial oligopoly, I didn't know where my *next* check was coming from, so, when I alighted from the Greyhound bus and noticed an all-night movie theater, to which the admission was only one dollar, I decided that I would pay my dollar, choose a seat toward the rear, and go to sleep.

"How often we fret over problems that go away of themselves! This was to prove just such a case: my next job was already waiting for me, had I but known, at the Homegrip Finance Corporation's office in Windsor, Ontario. For $200 a month, I would be entering homes and saying: "That's a nice TV, Mrs. Lesource, is it paid for? And how about that couch?" to distraught housewives who didn't know that in only 2% of all cases does HGF actually repossess. No, and I didn't know, when I purchased the mandatory hat, that it would come off as I was flung down some stairs one afternoon by a man in a T-shirt who was to come growling out of an inner room when Mrs. Lesource, who had assured me that Mr. Lesource was not at home, began to weep as I recited my lines.

"No, and I didn't know that the job I would have after I had quit HGF because of that, was to be as a door-to-door salesman peddling magazines at $5.50 commission per $29.95 contract." Here I must interpose that these revelations concerning our revered Master's youthful doings were distressing me considerably. Door-to-door salesman!—what next? By the time I had collected myself enough to attend to his words, I was horrified to hear him saying: "I shot her a dark, passionate glance. She thrilled as the hem of my trenchcoat brushed against the naked nylon of her leg. Would she sacrifice all for a few dizzying moments of risk beside the iridescent sea in the lean, suave embrace of the ship's captain?" Actually, this last part mystified more than it horrified. But then our Master went on: "That sort of writing is paid well; the system wishes to distract attention from itself, and that was the function of these magazines—that, and to bring news of products to the consumers. Part of the deal included a free dictionary that I priced at $54.95 when I quit that company. The cost was entirely covered by the sale of advertisements! Our manager, Lonnie, told me to say to the housewife, 'You don't want your kids to grow up as ignorant as you are, do you?' He had me memorize this; when I repeated it before the other crewmembers, I realized they were laughing at something besides my accent. Lonnie was a barrel of laughs. What I actually had to say was, 'You want your children to have all the advantages you didn't, I'm sure.'

"When Lonnie let me off on a block of tumbledown shanties, unkempt lawns littered with broken tricycles, and I demurred, and he with vehemence said to me 'You know *why* I'm giving you this territory? You know *why* these people don't have a pot to piss in? You know *why* they have all these kids? It's because they can't say No, that's why!' I confess that I appreciated the crude artfulness of his reasoning, and believed him. He was the better salesman.

"But all that was the Future. Meanwhile, I had installed myself in a warm, dry movie theater, sheltered from the midnight rain. I settled back into my seat and prepared to sleep. After the manner of the young, I did this by day-dreaming: here was the millionaire's daughter half-crazed with love of me; here was the million-dollar invention I couldn't quite see behind the stacks of hundred-dollar bills on my inventor's table; here was the estate in California with its swimming pool in the shape of Marilyn Monroe. . . . I had been in North America for some time already. Soon I was asleep and really dreaming. I was really dreaming I was being shaken violently: I wasn't dreaming, I really was being shaken violently, by a young man about my own age who now shone a flashlight in my face and said, 'Hey, buddy, you can't sleep in here.'

"I could not believe my ears. Nor, when I looked around, my eyes. These, by now able to penetrate the smoky gloom, aided by the light reflected from the huge screen, brought me depressing information concerning the caliber of person with as sharp an eye for a deal as myself. Many of them had brown paper bags, which they raised to their lips; all were men, most were unshaven. And passing among them, up and down the aisles, were other young men with flashlights. The advantage we had thought to take of this deal had been anticipated. Whoever slept, was shaken.

"But at what cost? What could be the turnover, at 3 A.M.? Would those of us too bored to watch the movie for the second or third time, go out into the street, and if so, was there really a line of men out there impatient to occupy our seats? What made it worth the management's while to keep all these young men in uniform and on active service?"

Our Master paused at this point; I understood he did this for effect, but a new member of our group, supposing the question required him to come up with an answer, called out: "A city ordinance?" Our Master regarded him steadily for a few seconds and then said, "Yes.

"But non-compliance with that ordinance was possible, I saw;

an usher passed by every twenty minutes or so; a night's sleep could be pieced together, quarter-hour by quarter-hour, given persistence in humiliating amounts. And in between, one had the screen to watch: one had to watch the screen.

"I began to watch the screen. It was a John Wayne movie. Or, I think, two. Because sometimes when I woke up he was wearing a cavalry uniform, and other times, a cowboy uniform; and sometimes he was killing Mexicans, and sometimes he was killing Indians. Of course," our Master said, with that concern that we should understand things American as precisely as he did, "he was not really killing them, and they were not really Mexican or Indian; merely actors who looked less American than John Wayne. And as for death, there was more real death in the alley behind the theater, which was one consideration kept us in there.

"My children," our Master addressed us with uncommon earnestness, "do not let you go as America went! All my ministry is this. I entertain you with a narrative. How neatly one piece fits into the piece that went before! The repetition of elements allows a sense of security. You are conducted to strange worlds fabulously furnished without any advance payment. You are reminded of something. You are supplied with a big picture to look at: a patio by night, a beachscape, the Alamo—for that was the name of the movie theater in Detroit. I encode a message for you to decipher; the culture has always rewarded you for succeeding in this activity. You feel superior, accomplished. But nothing has changed.

"It is easier to see through my little tales than it is to see through the pernicious society we are trapped within. But the difference is merely scale."

A gong sounded from deep inside the dwelling and my Master, after the briefest of pauses, said: "And speaking of that, the brownie of Death is already in us. Our consciences are encased in helmets of words. We are somewhere between sleep and waking, some of us" (and here he pointed a finger at Kay Elle, the renowned film critic) "so stupefied that we consider seriously, in the name of the people, pabulum as art; and when our masters wake us, it is only to make us witness their mendacities. We feel guilty for the furniture we cannot afford. It is ours, already, all of it, ours! When will we toss them down the steps so that their hats come off, preferably with their heads still inside? My children, there are so many of us, so very few of them! What do you have to say for yourselves?"

We were all far too embarrassed to speak. With a contemptuous wave of the hand, my Master indicated the way out.

I was the last to leave and, as I was buttoning up my jacket, my Master approached and laid his hand on my shoulder. "How else shall I validate my existence—let alone yours?" He paused, then resumed: "You ask me why the question even comes up? You would recommend to me a course of meditation? My friend, I have practised meditation in many forms. Invariably, the following happens: I study my navel. Hours or minutes pass in this fashion. Eventually, with a downward wipe (or sometimes by a kind of Dunning and Schufftan process), *my* navel is replaced by the protuberant, fatal navel of a starving child. You know, the way they look, when they show documentaries about capitalism on TV? This child is starving because the land its parents, in common with their fellows, used to farm has been stolen by a multimillionaire expropriator. Next, the navel dissolves into a beautiful fountain of white marble; gracious jets play from its several openings, to fall into a pond resplendent with *Nelumbo nucifera,* with the characteristic large leaves, fragrant, pinkish flowers, and broad, rounded, perforated seed pods. Now, by a kind of tilting and panning process, I see this fountain plays in the center of a courtyard paved with huge, asymmetrical flagstones of various colors; these have recently been hosed down, and sparkle and glitter in the brilliant mid-morning sun.

"Next, a long shot reveals the courtyard is surrounded on all sides by a profusion of flowers and shrubs: I grow aware of their many scents mingling in the heavy, honeyed air; and my ears fill with the immemorial humming of bees in innumerable bells. A series of tracking shots discloses something of the variety of plant-life: there are borders of lavender, behind which the mixed blues of delphiniums rise to create a delightfully soothing effect; here and there, at their feet, the yellow bursts of *Santolina naeapolitana.* There are borders of lychnis, asters, lysimachias, geraniums, heleniums and delphiniums, pink, blue, scarlet, yellow and white. There are borders of verbenas, tagetes, nicotianas, antirrhinums and pelargoniums, brilliantly yellow and red, purple and orange. There we see foxgloves, hollyhocks, and pink carnations. Here we see the white form of the grape hyacinth. Sweet-scented thyme, planted in tufts between the stones of the paths that invite one into the profusion, grows for the feet to trample; here are also pinks, whites and yellows—saxifrages and alpine phlox. And forget-me-nots and low-growing heathers have been effectively used as ground cover in this lovely corner—the perfect foil for the delicate coloring of the white violet rhododendron at the back. The pink and scarlet fuchsias, the blue, blue lobelias, trail from stone containers embedded in the walls that shelter this lovely spot from all unfavorable winds. A pergola, entwined with purple wisteria, abuts the rose-garden: of the hybrid teas alone, I can discern Chrysler Imperial, Eden Rose, Grace de Monaco, Lady Sylvia, Madame Butterfly, Symphonie and Silver Lining.

"To the east, an entire area of red, white and blue appears—the blues of Glory-of-the-snow (with its white eye), crocus, bluebells of England, primrose, flax, and the Virginia cowslip—or, if it is summer rather than spring, of the speedwells, the bellflowers, and the long, floriferous spikes of delphinia; the reds of crown imperial, barrenwort, tulips, fire-pink, lungwort, peonies, and the oriental poppy"—here my Master paused, having nearly stumbled over this last name—"and the whites! Ah, what whites! Narcissus, tulip, lily-of-the-valley, sweet william—snowdrops, sweet peas, peonies; and at one point, what is either goatsbeard or spirea, I can't quite decide; and, *pièce-de-résistance*, letters of baby's-breath on a background of snapdragons, spelling out the superb sentiment, 'No knowledge rightly understood can deprive us of the mirth of flowers.'

"Trained across the south-facing wall are nectarines and peaches. Beyond this wall lies the palace of the multi-millionaire. A green door in this wall opens, and through it steps a man in his middle years, of somewhat more than medium height, a rather spare figure in blue and golden robes of Nepalese cut, contrasting markedly with features almost occidental in their handsome strength, which make the long, wispy gray beard depending from his chin seem merely glued into place."

"But Master! The figure you describe is none other than yourself!" I could not help but exclaim. "Yes, indeed," my Master replied. "And I seldom looked happier, wouldn't you agree?

"But I'm doing all right, wouldn't you say?" He continued, before I could decide upon an answer. "Behind that curtain is a giant color TV. I loathe and despise myself for watching it. Therefore, in this drawer here, I keep a pipe, and some opium. Finest grade. It cost me a pretty penny too, I don't mind telling you!

"As soon as you have left (which I trust will be very shortly, as my tolerance for human company has reached the end of its tether), I shall wheel out the set, turn it on, recline on this rug in front of it, smoke a pipe, and pray that the drug take over my faculties before the first commercial comes on. Don't forget," he called as I was crossing the threshold for what at that moment I feared would be the last time, "next meeting, the next monthly fee is due! Tell the others!" Then the ornate door, with its embossed elephants, closed firmly behind me, and I was left to negotiate the steps in complete darkness.

UP FROM THE SUBTEXT

One Spring

It hailed. 0.06 inches were precipitated where the instruments are kept. At least one driver found his windshield wipers clogging. High winds drove the hail into the orchards of apple, pear & prune. It hailed on the new Vacu-Dry plant, an independent, publicly-owned corporation, making instant applesauce for the government. During the following night, thieves walked off with the bus-bench.

Next day samples were brought to the inspector. The leaves were shattered & the fruit already indented. Though the sun shone bright, some wisps of high cirrus appeared shortly after midday.

Next day dawned clear & bright, & by the middle of the afternoon the thermometer registered 73 degrees Fahrenheit. That night the valley-bottoms were free from frost. Next day began well also, the sky a clear deepening blue, the light flickering off the eucalyptus leaves.

At Goat Rock State Park, a man sat in a car, inhaling carbon monoxide. Sunset occurred at 6:35. The weather continued fine & warm for the remainder of the week. Some black lambs were gambolling in one green dell. Their dams had recently been shorn. The fence looked very old. It had been built by coolies in the last century. That night, a ring-tail cat showed up in a passing pair of headlights. The driver thought it was a raccoon. The ring-tail cat is neither cat nor raccoon, but more closely allied to the bear. It dropped to 44 that night; next day, it rose to 86.

The blue sky was no longer a strip, & beneath it the earth had risen grandly into hills—clean, bare buttresses, trees in their folds, & meadows & clear pools at their feet.

But the hills were not high, & there was in the landscape a sense of human occupation—so that one might have called it a park, or garden, if the words did not imply a certain triviality & constraint.

A person shopping at the market paid 89 cents for a pound of rib roast, 17 cents for a pound of cantaloupe. Corn cost the shopping person 49 cents for 5 ears; tomatoes were 2 for a quarter. Bob Thomson, who had been a ranger with the State Beach Parks Service for about 8 years, reported Monday to be Maintenance Coordinator for the River area of the State Park System.

This was a promotional transfer & he would be working with rangers along the coast also. There had been two suicides in the park last week, one at Goat Rock & one at Blind Beach.

All the new restrooms were in & the old ones were being removed. The warm weather had brought large crowds to the area over the weekend. It had been foggy Saturday & Sunday mornings but the ocean was fairly calm & boats were able to bring in good catches. Elsewhere, low tides two feet below the lowest on record concerned farmers, who feared a rise in salt-content of that water they employ in irrigation. "The tide is out," said Farmer Warner Tallman, "and as far as I can see, it'll never come back." This day the stock market finished lower, partly in reaction to the President's foreign policy message & partly the result of normal pre-weekend evening-up of pressures.

In late trading Burroughs, Walt Disney & Corning Glass were up a point or so apiece. The following morning was clear & sunny, with the fresh warmth of a full-summer day; the flowers were blossoming profusely & the grass was richly green. A student was arrested early in the day after the car he was driving struck the State College Library.

A man who was stealing $250 from a service station made up a story: he worked there, & would say that he passed out after two gunmen forced him to take some capsules & beer. When he woke up, they had rifled the place.

He would be due for sentencing within three weeks, having entered guilty pleas to charges of filing a false felony report, & petty theft. Days passed, & a 31-y-o woman stabbed her sister-in-law to death in a bar on Tuesday evening.

Wind again last week & our hills were beginning to look brown. The grass had had a much shorter season—less feed for the sheep & an earlier fire hazard. They first began at 2 P.M. at the home of Jay Gutz. Gutz was pouring gasoline into the carburetor when the fuel ignited. All the electrical wiring was destroyed in the '58 Olds. 15 firemen responded to the fire which was extinguished within 10 minutes.

At 8:45 P.M. a '65 Olds caught fire at the Phillips 66 station. The ignition had been left on while the car was being worked on. The wiring under the dash & the hood was destroyed. This fire was out within 10 minutes also.

Between 11:15 A.M. & 3:15 P.M., a human being entered a residential structure, pried open another human being's dresser drawer & a tin box inside that drawer, & removed $8,800 in cash.

Taxpayers had not built a school, staffed & maintained it in order that children should echo the revolutionary clatter from the state colleges.

Fog came in sometime Saturday night & hung on all day Sunday but it was very warm & pleasant for gardening.

As soon as it got warm in the valley one noticed an increased interest in real estate at the coast. Fred Hill, recently hospitalized, returned home, able to get about again. The day dawned bright.

The pre-dawn light was green, a function perhaps of dust or even smog, over the valley eastward. Then bright orange, & then the rim of the sun appeared behind the mountain range that forms the eastern edge of the valley. Some people boating, swimming or fishing or otherwise visiting the river & perhaps also some other large creeks could have been startled to see a gigantic & nightmarish rat, as the animal is fully as large as a raccoon, brown like a rat with a long scaly tail, over two-thirds of its body & headlength. It has very glossy yellowish-brown to dark-brown fur, which is actually a silk-like & waterproof under-fur, & which is covered on the outside by colorless guard-hairs, that you do not see.

The enormous hind feet, about 6 inches long, are heavily clawed & widely webbed. After the first shock of seeing it wears off & you begin to realize that even large as it is it is still hardly large enough to attack & eat a man, the observer is inclined to say, "O well, just another animal!"

But it is not just another animal, creeping silently inland & tearing up whole plants.

That afternoon, a skindiver fell off a rock & stabbed himself in the side with a fish spear. It was a relief that the wound proved not fatal. County Coroner Nigel Bruce had his work cut out for him. He continued to investigate a blaze that claimed the lives of two men early Tuesday.

Killed in a cabin fire on the Klein ranch were Hank Leith, 39, & Albert Ross, 22.

Bruce said the pair had apparently driven another couple from the cabin on the Klein ranch earlier that night. The blaze began around 4:30 A.M. The weather for the weekend was overcast but quiet. They had been using a kerosene lamp.

Sunday the wind came up & blew the fog away for a while. Pat Manzer reported the lupine at Duncan's Landing was beautiful this year. Her friend, Birnie Reid, answered that we were fortunate along the coast that we had wildflowers from early spring through summer. The rose cactus in the gardens were blooming this year with their tall stalks of small, starry, yellow blooms. At grange last week Mrs. Dewar had used these blooms with some nasturtiums & an orange cactus blossom to make decorations for the hall.

The seasons must be changing. Here it was June & we were having a very heavy mist called rain. While it would do some "rejuvenating" of the springs from which our drinking water comes, it would also damage some of the fruit crops. So it was a bright day for the wedding. The home was decorated for the occasion with spring bouquets. That afternoon the couple carved their initials in the family birch tree.

It was the bright day they had hoped it would be, had feared it would not be, those performing in the school auditorium: Roy Cooper with a yo-yo demonstration; Pat Dixon, Dave Robertson, Peter Burnet, vocal trio; George Palmerini, acting out a memory skit; Mrs. Peacock presenting a driver-training monologue; Toby Oldfield's class, performing their skit, Space People of Grade Ten. More performances were being planned.

Elsewhere, students paid tribute to police officers. The Student Body President said, "We know the police are getting a pretty raw deal at Berkeley & other state colleges. If it wasn't for their courage & dedication we might not have a college to attend when we graduate from high school." Two sounds rent the peace of the day.

According to Highway Patrol reports, the car, westbound, went out of control & hit a mailbox. The other was a shot of some light-bore gun. A 14-y-o boy had accidentally shot a younger boy in the foot with a BB gun. The wound in the bottom of the foot was not deep, Timmy's mother later reported. But she was frightened that next time he might be hit in the eye.

Young Ernie told police that the wound was unintentional. The shot may have ricocheted. Police took Ernie's BB gun & gave him a lecture. It is illegal to discharge firearms within city limits.

A young teacher named Lord had informed the school board that his free time, which the board had so graciously donated to the outdoor education project without asking Lord, or offering him any type of extra compensation, if you ignored a few quarters' worth toward gas mileage (Lord drove a Ford), was no longer at the board's disposal. To work beyond his contract, went on Lord, would require the board pay Lord time & a half above his hourly rate, & double time on the Lord's Day & other holidays, which they could well afford. "This is after all no more than any plumber asks," said Lord. "Board member Silas Broad, who voted for my ouster, is a plumber—for the record." They were floored. They thought it highly untoward. Broad waved a sword. In the afternoon, it poured.

Night fell & nocturnal animals left their burrows & nests to steal abroad—some for the last time. Some motorists slowed at the sign "Deer Crossing"; by others, it was overlooked. In those areas the fog reached in to this night, it gathered in the stands of eucalyptus & Monterey cypress &, condensing, dropped like rain (the fog). From Washington, where it was tomorrow already, word came of the first major contract to be awarded on the 80 million dollar dam project. Work was to begin almost immediately.

The next day I woke very early. The sun had only just risen; there wasn't a single cloud in the sky; everything around shone with a double brilliance—the brightness of the fresh morning rays & of yesterday's precipitation. I went for a stroll about a small orchard, now neglected & run wild, which enclosed the little lodge on all sides with its fragrant, sappy growth. On the slope of a shallow ravine, close to the hedge, could be seen a beehive; a narrow track led to it, winding like a snake between dense walls of high grass & nettles, above which struggled up, God knows whence brought, the pointed stalks of dark-green hemp.

Those of us who remembered the May stabbing at Pete's Bar noted that Mavis Baker, 29, was pleading innocent to murder. Rosa Quintero, 33, died in the hospital with a 9-inch butcher knife in her back. It was stuffy in the courtroom. The heart of the city had been rendered barren by a recent earthquake. We were glad to be home.

Fred Hill's daughter visited Sunday at the Hill house. A week before, Mrs. Hill and daughter, Mrs. Ann Livingston, met two women friends from Weed, and all four drove to Lake Tahoe for the remainder of the week. Mrs. Hill returned home Friday evening. They chatted persistently in familiar tones. Few realize that their life, the very essence of their character, their capabilities & their audacities, are only the expression of their belief in the safety of their surroundings. The courage, the composure, the confidence; the emotions & principles; every great & every insignificant thought belongs not to the individual but to the crowd: to the crowd that believes blindly in the irresistible force of its institutions & of its morals, in the power of its police & of its opinion.

After a few drizzly days the wind came up Saturday night, & Saturday turned out to be a howler of a day with lots of white caps on a rough ocean. The Liberty Belle, a fishing boat owned & operated by Quincy Brigg of La Jolla, burned in the channel Tuesday morning.

It was a fairly calm morning & the smoke could be seen for quite a distance, so those coming down the coast early that morning knew something was wrong before they reached the bay. An electrical plug apparently ignited the boat's gasoline engine.

With the white cardboard boxes held high above her head, & with her robe open, flapping behind her, a young woman leaped high & for a moment seemed to float above the top strands. She landed running. Pieces of her white robe adhered to the wire barbs.

Along the side of the country lane, back where her car was parked, a county employee was mowing the wildoat grass. He was turning over in his mind a report he'd read that morning at breakfast. Narcotics & drugs were the health topics of greatest concern to local residents. "How to understand the Bible" had been the most often checked Bible topic in the survey conducted by the Christian Brotherhood Church. 23.7% had checked that one.

21.5% had checked "Why so many churches?"; 17.5% had checked "What does God expect?"; 15.7% had checked "Life after Death"; 15%, "How to Pray"; 15% "What Is Faith?"; 13.6% wanted to know about "Money & the Church"; 12.5% were curious as to "World situation & prophecy"; 12.5% also wondered, "Is the Devil real?"

The other health topics had been, & in this order of concern: Prevention of heart attacks, What can be done about cancer, Help for arthritis, Tips on gardens, Weight control, Mental health, Nervous breakdown, Help for smokers, Emergency first aid, Physical fitness, Ulcers. Sweat ran into his eyes.

Concentration was required, to keep the blade from shattering on a concealed roadside rock. He was allergic to pollens, & wore a kerchief across mouth & nose, like a bandit. Across a small flat meadow some careful rancher had tied strips of white cloth to his barbwire fence, to prevent people from walking into it in the dark. A Volvo was abandoned directly in his path.

Raising the blade, he drove around the foreign body, then, lowering his instrument, resumed cutting. The kingfisher spies a fish or frog in the water or on the bank & dives down to seize it. He will often fly straight down into the water like a flying spear.

The dipper, on the contrary, either walks about over the rocks in a shallow part of the stream, picking up with his bill the insects he finds, or may calmly dive down into a pool & walk along the bottom & over the rocks picking up insects & eating them right there, not later. Such soft greens & grays, after the hot white days! It's a strange thing that when the fog comes in it seems to deaden all the normal sounds except the bird calls. Hi's & lo's for this week: 52/100 — 57/104 — 58/106 — 55/93 — 49/81 — 47/79 — 47/76 (Wednesday thru Tuesday). It is worth noting that the weather records for the City are actually kept by a person who lives on Green Valley Lane, 4 miles outside city limits, & where the range in temperature tends to be greater than in our town. The end of Main Street is looking good.

Superior French Laundry folks painted their building. Safeway is always super clean & probably one of their finer stores. Goodsports & Ernie's Liquors reflect modern merchandising techniques, & so does Robbie's Grill. All doubtless show significant growth in revenues. The Pine-Cone Café will be a collector's item one day. Owners keep their store areas clean & neat. Who wants to wade through litter & debris to enter a store?

Pretty Proserpine Thomson, 14, the daughter of Mr. & Mrs. Robert Thomson, is examining a basket of plump, ripe raspberries at the handsome Goatz Ranch on Green Hill Road.

Up from the Subtext

for C.B. and N.L.

As they reach the crest of the dunes, the parking lot behind them, the ocean and its beach in front of them, he sees, looking in the direction they are going to take, a jeep, coming this way. They let it pass, assuming, correctly, a ranger to be driving it. When it has vanished in the haze to the north they feel free to slide down to the beach, their (forbidden) dog with them. They find the hard sand and set off at a good pace, south.

The adults walk at a regular pace; the two boys come and go, as the dog, their attentions pulling them this way and that. The waves move in on their right; the dunes continue on their left. The beach is strewn with sea-wrack, weathered logs, jellyfish, at one point a dead seal, headless. They call the dog off. Fog closes in, thick enough to curl the woman's hair and soften the man's beard. The boys are aglow, their boots, despite the man's repeated cautions, soaking.

Three figures appear ahead, on the left, coming across their own projected trajectory, presumably toward the ocean. One of the boys says he hopes they're all right. The man calls the dog to him and leashes him, thinking to make him seem more fierce. Close up, the two young men and the young woman open like flowers. That is to say, the baffling air of menace vanishes, they are plainly enthused with the place, all smile and exchange greetings, and soon they are left behind.

The headland looms up in the fog. Now it's been reached the boys discover what the adults, who have visited this place before, had not told them, that a small cave opens in its base. The boys want to explore it, then, inside its entrance, don't. The man chooses to attend to the fascination of it and not to the

95

repulsion he also feels, and the others follow him. It extends into the cliff only some dozen feet. He can just stand upright. The walls, sandstone, are glistening with seepage. A trickle of clear water emerges from a crack by his head and runs to a groove in the floor, thence out into the cove.

They leave the cave and climb the headland. It's a comfort to walk on solid ground, and, after the scramble up the loose sandy earth, along the level. Some twisting shrub, knee-high, is everywhere in evidence, and marks where the trail leads. At the tip of the headland it's possible to climb out onto a kind of jagged table of rock, dotted with tide-pools, and this they do. Every three or so minutes a series of three or four huge waves rolls in, shooting spray maybe twenty feet into the air over their heads, drenching them. The rocks resound with the impact. Where the ocean has worked deep gullies in the rocks, water shoots up at amazing speed. The boys enjoy being scared; the balance, of risk and safety, is perfect. The adults are not so sure. Or surer. The man would enjoy *this* place more were the boys not in his care. But wouldn't be here. The dog, too, is a worry. To what extent can he be assumed prescient, as to the potential risks he runs in jumping around from point to point in such a place?

Two pelicans fly low overhead while the party of four eats lunch. Two medium-size birds, black, with orange bills, pass with shrill pipings, turn just before landing, land. Are they black terns, the adult couple wonders. Further along, as the four of them follow the narrow path that skirts the cliff's edge, are many cormorants, looking like small seals, perched in crevices. There are places it would be possible to scramble down, but there's the walk back to conserve strength and energy for.

They decide it's time to turn back; a marine biology station blocks their way. They are already trespassing. In the fog, lying on their fronts in the short grass, they study the place. They draw parallels between this situation and those imaginable from TV situations. They are there to blow the space-station up. They are on another planet, and indeed they are. It is this one. On the walk back, the fog no longer yields intermittently to sunlight, they move ahead, the man thinks, and then remarks to the woman, in a kind of spheroid oval, they could be anywhere in the world where there

96

is such a beach. The waves are constant on their left; the sand-dunes on their right. They find several perfect sand-dollars. The man and the woman are walking hand-in-hand now. The boys have worn themselves out by, for example, twirling long sea-weeds around their heads like lariats, and by the generally erratic nature of their movement, which, at age nine, neither has the experience to control for long toward some end, however desirable. They fall back, and when the man or the woman turns to see how they're doing, look woebegone.

They brighten up somewhat when a vulture and two ravens are discerned in wait by the corpse of the seal. But these birds fly off before the party can get as close as it would like. The dog runs very fast when he sees snipe or sandpipers or gulls along the water's edge, but they rise casually and move out over the water, so the dog turns in a half-circle and canters back, his tongue lolling. Looks like a wry grin. The exercise, the adults agree, is good for him.

Here is a dead cormorant, freshly dead, for its corpse looks to be in good condition. It has blue eyes! Such a blue! Its blackness is actually a dark brown, but its feet are black-brown too, and its long bill, but its little eye is blue as blue can be.

They see people ahead of them, up the beach. The man and the woman will ask them if we are anywhere near the parking lot, for the dunes block all view beyond them to the east. The man approaches the six or seven youngsters, who sit in a companionableness he thinks might be stoned, and one or more of them point just behind them, Sure, right here. They grin pleasingly, and it feels good to be grinning with them. Now, the goal almost reached, the boys give up, flinging themselves down in the sand as if wishing they were a couple of years younger, and could therefore expect to be carried the remaining 200 yards. But they soon come to their senses and so the crest is reached and the dog races ahead of them to circle the familiar car.

DOWN FROM THE MOUNTAIN

"He Was"

He was to go into his feelings that he avoided so adroitly with
thought. When he asked his thought for a picture he was shown
the crawl-space underneath the house, where he had never been
and where he had no intention of going if he could possibly help
it. Going into it a little further he found there were cobwebs against
his face, spiders he couldn't quite see, and knew these were only
tokens of what wouldn't present itself in the picture. He sat in
the living room, lit by four standing lamps of considerable
elegance, astutely placed, both for use and for effect; the hardwood floor shone, the furniture made all kinds of sense. Leave
this for the darkness and confusion that, by being underneath,
in a sense made *this* room possible?

Now he was arguing towards a glimpsed conclusion, moving
a lamp a little nearer to his questioner's person, wanting, he
remarked, to see her better, and coincidentally dazzling her. If
that place made this one possible, then hadn't he made the right
decision, to experience it *here,* to stay where he was, leaving the
other area to be the living room of what more properly dwelt
there—black imaginary widows and, in short, the unthinkable?

Yet he was intrigued with what she had to present, and this
argued a certain pain, for if utter satisfaction were his, wouldn't
he fall asleep—wouldn't he be, already, asleep? Still, if this was
a dream, it was one that pressed toward its end. If you hurt bad
enough, a memory of a friend who had started to be shrunk told
him, you go. But it was *his* notion that madness inhered in
deliberately going out, into the night, then down the steps and
on his hands and knees to crawl through the darker veil that was
the entrance, down there. Sooner or later, he knew, he would get
up to cross this floor and it would simply give way beneath him,
not because it was rotten but because it was a picture, and you

can't walk about in a picture. He would be plunged into the underneath before he had to think about it and that would be that. Nothing left to do at that point but scream.

But this would probably not happen today, or even this week. He would suffuse himself with terror, screaming for help and screaming at anyone crazy enough to try to pull him out. So in this way too he would not have to look at the crawl-space.

He now thought this was not only beneath him in space but behind him in time, and so far back that his success at survival throughout the years argued against the necessity of exploration. But she now drew to his attention the fact that, upstairs, there was another crawl-space. So the house, which looks so spacious from outside, is, as far as its liveable portions go, almost cramped.

Was it love, he wondered, made him listen to this uncomfortable guest—if, first and last, love for himself? But love is blind so why not stay put or, say, move the whole show into the next room, where the bed was. The sexual charge was a welling up of the otherwise inadmissable—so he had conceived. What if he were to enter his own crawl-space with a cool expectation of suffering—suffering all corners and each fold with a deliberation possibly passionate but divorced from the enchantment he desired to feel but that was, after all, only a web of thought—for such, he figured, was fantasy. In fantasy also he saw what memory called Th'expense of spirit in a waste of shame. But love! he balked, closing his eyes. These were his own lids, naturally, over his own eyeballs.

One must love from strength not weakness. He opened them up and looked into hers, green where there is color to be refused but, as everywhere, darkly open at center. The hero has a thousand faces but he would be all alone in the basement. Is it weak to want to fuse one's being with another's. Were the pictures on these walls to relieve the monotony or was analogy one more evasion.

The fact of it is, there is two thousand dollars' worth of dryrot under this house, and somebody is going to have to do something about it. But it's all a fiction since I sit here writing of it, and facts do not enter such writing without undergoing transformation. There is the time of writing having energies specific to itself

102

that preoccupation by what earlier occurred transgresses. Thinking this made him uneasy. Calling himself *him* helped, if only from a distance. She sat, after all, some little distance from him. And upstairs, when one came to read this, it would be the same.

If he sat in the room, wasn't that what he had to confront—sitting there trying not to be filled with the other place. There, he would not be able to look at her, and her visible presence was part of her persuasiveness. She had persuaded him to recognize the act that charged his feelings so—it was something done to him so terrible, so heartrending, that it was unavengeable. He would do anything to revenge himself, he thought, and thought—thinking, that the child was someone he no longer was, it had been done to another person altogether. He was crying, suddenly, grief forcing itself up from the darkness in his chest, blurring his eyes. But you are crying for yourself, he imagined she had said. And the light was back.

Unwinding the Wound

The initial wrench is sickening, unbelievable. How can this be happening to me. Maybe it's a defense against this to remember it, within a very short time, as utterly predictable, the inevitable culmination of a fateful series of acts. Possibly one will believe one willed it.

The pain is such that one won't want to move from the place where it happened, & will hug the hurt, pulling it into oneself. But it's most quickly alleviated if you get up & walk so that the injured part is forced to function. Soon only a sinister clicking within predicts the next stage.

Which is, a growing soreness & intractability, that will fix it in whatever position one adopts, which will usually be sitting, discussing how it happened probably, so that it grows increasingly difficult to straighten it out. But it must be straightened out in order to be bound so one can get around.

But more immediately, extreme cold affords relief. Something like an ice-pack, administered by a cool-headed friend, whose attentions may also ease the ego, which is wounded because one has been foolish enough to have this accident at all. The swelling however makes the friend hard to attend to.

Then it must be bound. This is what is always done in such cases. Which means that many, many others have had to endure pain of this kind. And they are now walking around okay, so, recovery looks to be highly probable. This bandage, which has to be elastic, supports the injured member & diminishes feeling therein.

But not entirely. At night, particularly, the efforts, to accommodate oneself to the hurt, place unaccustomed strain on other areas, making sleep as difficult as it is desirable. In the half-awake half-asleep state one may wonder whether these secondary pains aren't the cause of the first.

But one will wake up & start to think again. One may see how the incident could have been avoided. If the pain gets too intense one has recourse to drugs. One recalls how it has happened as it happened & it's best to forget all that entirely. One recalls friends who were intensely into drugs.

A doctor will draw off the excess fluid with a hollow needle, hollow because it's to be filled with one's own effluent. He won't use anesthetic, because the patient must advise him whether the needle is probing into the fluid, or the injured tissue itself. This shrinking procedure doesn't guarantee that fluid won't gather again. Then the procedure must be repeated. What's more, the doctor's bill will be repeated. And the doctor may not know what he is doing.

Twenty-four hours have passed. Now the compresses should be changed from cold to hot. Hot pads hasten the re-absorption back into the general body, of the blood & lymph instrumental in the swelling. Gentle massage may do the same. But if the injured member is subjected in this way to any stress, it will give way immediately.

After a while the patient will have found various ways of thinking about all this. I was trying to get to first base & I did, but I forgot it's the one base you're allowed to overrun, so I tried to stop there, & part of me did, but part kept right on going. Equally, everything one thinks of, to cover it up, will bring the wrench to mind.

As the experience enters one's repertoire, one will be able to advise others likewise afflicted. But the distance between one & one's own pain, a distance that increases of necessity, if one's ever to trust the injured part, must take something away from these sympathetic efforts. Little more appears possible than to state that softball has rules, & that a knee, also, is a working set of limitations.

A knee has limitations inherent in its function. It's a joint, where two bones are bound together by an unlikely cluster of tendons. These enable the leg to go places neither the calf nor the thigh could get to on their own. And when thigh & calf must go their separate ways, these can tear.

You and Your Reasons

You must have had quite a journey of it, bringing those reasons of yours all these many miles! But it will prove to have been worth it, for you will have much need of them.

On the evening when your four-year-old child points at the moon! the moon! snared in this plane tree as it was snared in the previous one the two of you passed under, and tells you the moon is following you.

On the night when your lover asks you just what it is that keeps you hanging around. After all, you can't simply shrug and say that it beats watching paint dry.

In the morning when you are not getting up for work. The reasons your father gave you for getting up for work no longer prove sufficient. After all, *you* could go on unemployment, or turn to crime. *He* couldn't. So you will need some of the finest reasons from some of the best books, which is why we sent you to college. You need reasons that can outlast your cynicism, which is not really yours but merely a sign of the times. Complicated literary reasons are the best—you cannot possibly see through them before you have showered and broken your fast and dressed and by that time you might as well go because the money's not all that bad.

And you will need your reasons socially, as you will find that your deductive and inductive powers provide excellent entertainment for others.

You are at these people's place one evening, say, and they are the parents of a woman you met in London when you were mixed up with that theatre crowd you had reasons for hanging out with then, in those days. And the woman is there too, the young woman, the woman who must be 24 or so but who seems younger than her years, curiously arrested in her development, and never more so than this evening, back in her parents' home in San Francisco. You are there with your spouse, so this is not a tale of covert passions, unless of course they are very covert, so covert you haven't taken them into account until this very minute.

Anyway, you offer to fetch the beans from the kitchen—everyone being now seated at the dining table—and as you enter the kitchen you see the saucepan lid rise straight up in the air for about two feet, and then not so much fall as be flung violently to the floor. It makes a huge clatter. You hear exclamations from the other room. You go back out there with the beans and say, as casually as you can, "Oh, that? I just witnessed a poltergeist manifestation, that's all. The saucepan lid rose three feet straight up in the air and then fell forcefully as if flung to the floor."

Then there is a long silence. Then everybody begins talking at the same time, as if to cover up the fact of poltergeistism among them, your hosts, and you and your spouse, their guests. You think to yourself, "This is what humans do, cover up the threatening and the out-of-control with a web of words," but you also have to think, "They're embarrassed to have a mad hallucinated person visiting them and eating beans off their dining table."

Ann and Dan Got Married

Life is a rose-garden. The petals
wilt and the thorns remain.
—Fritz Perls

Ann *wants Daddy. But Mommy has beaten her to it.*

Ann liked it that Danny was older. Oh, not old enough to be her father. But he was promising material. She would make him into a fair replica of *a* father.

Ann would do this by acting younger than her age. By pretending not to understand what she was doing. She would invite this unhappily married man back to her flat for some classical music. She would be delightfully surprised to discover he was an amateur musician. Ann liked the way he played her piano. While he was thumping away, she would surrender herself to the seductive notion that he was thumping away just for her.

Ann never ceased to act girlish around Dan. At first, when she was 19, this was charming.

To Ann, acting girlish meant acting more grown-up than she was, the way her father had wanted her to act when she was really and truly a girl. It meant tippy-toeing around so as not to upset Daddy or the Daddy-substitute. It meant not letting Daddy see her true negative feelings. It came to mean paying the bills and driving the car and fending off visitors. It came to mean acting sophisticated about relationships during the 70s, a dangerous time to try that kind of a bluff. It came to grief.

Dan *had* Mommy. Then Daddy kept coming back to take her away. But nevertheless, he had had her. It was Daddy he couldn't get to. So being handed a Daddy-role was attractive, possibly.

109

Especially when the Daddy was really a big baby who got everything done for him.

Dan didn't like to make decisions. He liked to blame this on the Post-Modern condition. But to everyone else it was apparent that this had more to do with Dan than with *Waiting for Godot* or a general confusion of social values. He should have to make the decisions *they* were faced with! Then he'd know Post-Modern!

Actually, Dan was good at decisions about ends. He had decided to quit his unhappy marriage and live by himself. But women wouldn't leave him alone. It was simply that there were more of them than there was of him. He couldn't decide to begin anything, though, so he was spared most of these potential entanglements.

So Dan liked it that Ann acted so decisive around him. She decided they should take their socks off and then go to bed together. When she came back to Berkeley from the obligatory summer in La Jolla, she decided she should move in with Dan, rather than look for her own apartment. And when Dan's landlady gave him notice, on the grounds that his extra-marital arrangement would corrupt her young children who lived just over his head, Ann decided that she and Dan should find a place together. She would do the looking and the finding. All Dan had to do was to pack up his books.

Ann doted on Dan. So of course he told her that he loved her, too. But secretly this made him uneasy. There were so many meanings to the word. He suspected that Ann meant it one way and that he meant it another way.

Part of the trouble was that Ann never would confront him. So he couldn't know what his feelings were. Ann didn't want him to know what his feelings were. She suspected he didn't really love her, not the way she loved him. She feared if he were to find this out that he might leave. Ann may not have been conscious of this, but Dan couldn't tell the difference anyway between people's conscious and unconscious motives. So he worried that he wasn't giving Ann enough reassurance. He felt like an ingrate, and redoubled his efforts. His charm cheered her up.

Ann and Dan had lots of fun. He would stand there talking

to himself under his breath and Ann would come and dance around them both, the muttering one and the hearkening one, and fuse them with her high spirits and curious ways. As time went by, Dan came to identify with Ann. Without usually intending to, he impersonated her. This drove Ann wild with desire. She could make love to herself without feeling lonely!

Of course, Ann was resentful that Dan left everything practical up to her, even though or maybe just because she encouraged him to do so. She complained about it, but never to him. She complained about him to her friend Fran. She complained that Dan treated her like a little girl. This only increased Ann's pleasure. She got to be treated like a little girl and, like a little girl, all she could do was complain about it in secret to her girlfriend.

Fran replied that it looked to her like Dan treated Ann like she was his Mommy. This too gave Ann pleasure, for now she had replaced her own Mommy in a relationship with her Daddy-substitute. Ann found it was even more fun to complain about this to Fran. For as long as she was complaining about her relationship to Dan, that she was his daughter or that she was his Mommy, she was enjoying in a reflective way what she otherwise enjoyed in a half-conscious way. In order to complain she had to name, and she liked to find names for these binds. The binds gave her a sense of still being a child, for they were arrangements she felt powerless to alter, while naming them gave her a sense of power over her life.

Yes, for all that she was unliberated and unhappy, Ann was eating and having her cake, and very tasty she found it. All around Ann women were waking up and confronting the tyrants they had been brainwashed into marrying but Ann pooh-poohed all that. Secretly she was afraid of it, afraid of catching the infectious new spirit that threatened to carry off the persona she felt so secure in. Why, one heard of cases where the fellow actually started to listen to reason and stopped throwing dishes and started to do them instead! This was not for Ann. She had cast herself in a role that suited her to a "T": she was one of those girl-heroines from Nineteenth-Century Literature whose mothers having died have Daddy all to themselves and pay the bills and the rent and keep the house so that Daddy can continue with his important work as an inventor of devices no one will ever see the use of except for the heroine herself.

This was the sort of Daddy Ann had made of Danny. It hadn't involved making him over entirely. Dan's mother and father and his first wife and the other women and men of his generation had all contributed. He could never have done it alone. Decades later, some men would claim that they had already been doing their share of the housework and childcare by this time in history, but usually they were lying, rewriting history to make themselves look better. They would claim that they had already stopped being promiscuous male chauvinists twenty years ago but this was just another line. They didn't say it to each other. They told it to women.

Dan was actually somewhat closer to seeing the light than many of his men friends during this the early-middle period of the relationship of Ann and Dan. While living alone he had gotten into doing the dishes and the laundry and messing around with food on his hotplate. However, after some years with Ann, who offered herself for each of these chores, he found it easier to backslide. If he *did* do the chores, Ann would invariably laugh at him, gently, and point out what was wrong with his methods. So it became easier to remain impractical.

When it came to childcare, though, Dan was almost in step with his time as it came later to be lyingly characterized. He saw his little son Van two or three times a week and would usually take him on a field trip of some kind, just the two of them. In fact Dan figured out that he spent more actual time with his son than *his* father had spent with him, although they had for the most part lived in the same house. Bit by bit Ann got herself included in these trips, and then, when Dan was under particular pressure because he had an opening coming up (for Dan's inventions were sculptures, and a handful of people found them interesting), Ann in the goodness of her heart would take charge of Van.

After Ann and Dan moved to the country, Ann would often drive to Berkeley to fetch or return Van to or from his mother's house. Dan couldn't drive; he abstained out of purely humanitarian

112

motives, on the grounds that he was too absent-minded to be in charge of such a weapon. Ann let Dan get away with this bullshit (which he believed) and so she had to do all the driving. But at least she had Dan where she wanted him and knew where he was at all times, unless someone else was taking him for a ride. Between his sculpting and his hobby, music, Dan had gotten to know a lot of people, and sometimes one of these good folk would come and fetch him in order to play with him.

But mostly he was at home, and usually Ann was there with him. They not only were together a lot, they did a lot of things together. They gardened together, they read Thomas Mann's mighty novel *Doktor Faustus* together, marveling at the associations of music with the diabolical, they read *The Odyssey* together (Dan was moved to tears by the part about being wrecked on Calypso's isle), they went skinny-dipping in the hippie pond together, they made love under the sun and under the stars together, they made friends together, they played with Van and his friends together, and pretty soon, Ann decided they should sculpt together and she started to sculpt.

Dan's pieces weren't the simplest in the world, and it often took a few viewings to decide just where the representation was buried in them, but Ann's pieces were grotesques and immediately apprehensible as such. At first she did bats and lizards and bugs but then she started to do human figures—a person going to the bathroom, an acquaintance falling downstairs, Lot's Wife being turned into a pillar of salt unable to stop looking back. They were right for the times and Dan was among the first to see this. He wrote to the owner of the gallery which showed most of his own work and sent photographs of Ann's art. The man was not convinced so Dan wrote him a long letter pointing out how Ann's work worked. And then the man was convinced, and gave Ann her first show.

One curious fact about Ann as a sculptress was that she seldom could figure how to finish a piece. To Dan it was usually quite obvious and he would tell her how to if she asked him to.

About this time Dan began composing songs. They weren't very good, although he had some terrific talents to help him. His favorite was about a man who is able through magical powers to shrink himself to a height of six inches and ride around in his wife's pocket. From time to time she slips her hand in there and feeds him pieces of chocolate. Then she has a bra specially made and carries him around in that, and when people come to call, she produces him and sets him on the table where he speaks in a thin voice barely within the range of human audition. But it doesn't matter that the neat American sentences he utters can't be decoded: it's enough that this diminutive figure speaks at all. Then she has a miniature piano made for him, and her friends enjoy watching him tickle its ivories.

As a song, it sank beneath the weight of its details, and Dan soon returned to sculpting. As a clue that the marriage was headed for trouble, it was indecipherable to those it most concerned.

Yes, Ann and Dan had finally married. Dan hadn't seen the need for it but Ann had shown him that once they moved to the country she could no longer pretend to her parents that she was living with a female room-mate, as she had done during the Berkeley years. Besides, hadn't Dan complained about the inconvenience, having to move out whenever her folks came to town? He had had to go stay in Fran's flat while Fran and a large part of her wardrobe (enough to hide Dan's things in the closets) had to move into Dan and Ann's place. Dan let Ann know he thought it was dumb to go through this farce in the 1970s but Ann knew she could never let her parents know that she was living in sin no matter what decade they were in. They would think Ann was decadent.

First comes love, then comes marriage, then comes someone with a baby-carriage. Ann repeated this truth to Dan until he got sick of hearing it. It didn't take long. He was convinced that he was inadequate parent material. He said that, like many cursed with the artistic temperament, he was childish and egocentric and had no room in his life for another baby. But Ann pointed out that he already had had another baby, whereas she, Ann, had not, and that this was unfair. Dan could sometimes be won over by an appeal to his sense of fair play.

But not on this matter. What would have been the upshot

if Ann had told him, Either we have a child, or I'll leave you? Who can say? Ann did not have the nerve to find out. So something else happened instead.

What happened instead depends upon whether it is told by a friend of Ann or a friend of Dan. In one version, Ann sends a urine sample to a doctor friend who tests it on a rabbit and discovers Ann is pregnant. Ann retails this news to Dan who asks her to have an abortion. Ann just happens to have to go into hospital for this operation while Dan is away showing his art. When Dan phones that night, Ann tells him the doctors in the hospital found out it was a false pregnancy.

In the other version, Ann tries to bluff Dan into thinking she is pregnant, in the hope that he will be overjoyed at the news. Then Ann and Dan will copulate without further precautions and Ann *will* get pregnant.

Later, when they heard from Ann how miserable she had been in this marriage, how tired she had gotten of doing all the housework and of driving the car and of Dan's musical sessions, how tiresome had been his tantrums, how depressing his unwillingness to procreate, Ann and Dan's friends were quite startled. True, they had glimpsed problems, had understood that the marriage was not as ideal as Ann at the time had pretended; but they had also watched Ann's pleasure in being with Dan, the pleasure she took in making his friends hers, the pleasure she took in Dan's art and her own, the pleasure she took in making music with Dan and friends; it was difficult, later, to hear that this show of pleasure was due solely to Ann's consummate ability as an actress. It looked more likely to be a case of history rewritten to gain sympathy *post facto* for the rewriter. Dan thought this was a great idea.

If Ann had learned from her marriage, these friends agreed, she would not have spoken of her new husband, Stan, as the Real Mr. Right. While this implied that Dan had been the False Mr. Right, it also implied Ann's continuing belief in the fiction of a Mr. Right. It had been Ann's belief in this fiction when applied to Dan that had helped destroy the relationship, some held, because it placed too great a burden on Dan's slender shoulders. Just as, however much broader Stan's frame, it placed too great a burden on him, which made Ann's friends worry about her.

No, Ann and Dan had had a great deal of fun together, and if Ann chose to regard this as misguided in her later incarnation, she couldn't quite erase that truth from her memory. Proof of this were the figures she was still making, ten years after the divorce, grotesques no doubt, but recognizably of Dan, keeping the connection to her past lover alive even while, in the apparent fury of their genesis, invoking his destruction.

When friends mentioned this to Dan, he agreed, saying that he himself often harked back to those days, which, if only that they preceded by some fifteen years the present in which the world was being turned into a labor camp, looked golden, thronged with friends who had nothing better to do than to hang out, play music, and talk sculpting. Ann was a remarkable woman and he wished her well. He thought her art had fallen off, her grotesques were no longer amusing but sentimental or despairing, and they had an unfinished look about them. He felt bad for the way he had used her life, given that she had later complained of this; but she might have spoken up at the time, Dan felt.

The trouble was, when Ann, egged on by new female acquaintances, *did* begin to object to Dan, it was much too late; he had become accustomed to an unobjecting mate. He could only regard her novel ways as aberrant. He withdrew.

The last days were dismal enough. Dan no longer wanted to play piano, or even blues harmonica. He didn't sculpt much any more. Mostly he smoked—watched tv and smoked. He had smoked so much that his neck had gotten just like a turkey's, the way the necks of people who smoke a lot almost always do. And he had circles under his eyes from his swim-goggles, for swimming was another habit he indulged in at this time, even persuading Ann to take it up. For a while it was good for her figure, for which at the time Ann was grateful to Dan, as she had been years before when he talked her into giving up her wiglet and letting her hair grow out into a gorgeous aureole. But once she gave up smoking, Ann, who did not give up being oral, put on weight so that, if Dan resembled an old gobbler, Ann, whose neck never had been of the longest, came to look like another animal ritually slaughtered at holiday time.

It was only a matter of time before some fan of Dan's should

116

take Dan away from Ann. But within a year, Ann had met Stan. And seeing that had turned out so well, it was a puzzle that, after the initial pain and rancor dispersed, Ann had not become grateful to Dan for seeing how to end it and freeing her to meet the Real Mr. Right. But the paradox of the Fortunate Fall was beyond her.

Also beyond Ann's powers of forgiveness were any claims Van had on her love. She had become a good companion as well as a fine stepmother to Van, but after Dan left she would have nothing more to do with his son. Dan could understand some of Ann's meannesses after he left, just as he understood that those men who most wanted to leave their own wives, were those who most excoriated Dan for leaving his. (Later, these men left their wives.) He could understand those women who detested him in the name of sisterhood, just as he understood, later, when they called him up to ask how he was doing, and if he still missed Ann.

But Dan found harder to understand Ann's rejection of Van. When Van told Dan, Dan told Van it was probably that Ann needed to forget him (Dan) and that this probably had to mean forgetting Van too. But this was scarcely consolation for Van. Ann had been his friend. Now she treated him as if he were dead. Or as if she was.

So finally Dan determined to do a piece that would contain his feelings about Ann, and he went to work on it and worked for weeks, but he couldn't see how to finish it. Then he saw that it had to be done in Ann-style, but with more charity.

While he was working on it, he went several times to see the latest retrospective of her work: figures he had helped Ann finish, and figures no one had. These latter had an odd consistency. In each, the Dan-figure, curiously distorted and maimed, is discovered in the act of making something. Some thought this something resembled an Ann-like figure; others, that it resembled nothing human. Others pointed out that it was simply present to prop the Dan-figure up. They drew attention to other male figures, which they called Stan-figures, which had identical ill-defined shapes under their hands, likewise serving (if not doubling) as props. Many said they missed a woman figure standing on its own two feet. But Dan said all the figures looked like Ann to him.

Then Dan took a trip. His sculpture was on show in a remote town, so he went alone. He was put up at a motel and that night he called his wife, Penny, and let her sweet contralto soothe his nerves. As she spoke, he could picture her sitting at the phone table in the hallway. Her long brown hair flowed over her shoulders and her dazzling smile spoke into the mouthpiece. Or possibly she was mugging silent freakout at having to field his phonecall while trying to get the kid to bed or work on her files or watch tv. Her big blue eyes would be bugging out and her mouth fixed in a comic-strip scream. After they said goodnight and hung up, he sat at the desk in his room, remembering.

Penny always sounded so sensible, she wore a mask easily and wisecracked with the best of them. But once in a while the persona would let slip a glimpse of need—tonight, in the final five seconds, when she said "I love you, Daniel." She couldn't be too vulnerable around him: he would walk right in and assume the ancient male prerogatives.

Dan lay down on his left side and, hugging the pillow that would have been hers had she been with him, fell fast asleep.

When he woke, he didn't know what time it was, only that it was still dark. He was hungry. He found a bar of chocolate, ate it, and went back to sleep.

There was a waterfall, a canal, a fountain, a golf course, a house. It was his house, his and his wife's. But the woman in it was Ann. She was as she had been the summer when she had been her slenderest. Sun-bleached curls, slender ankles, golden down on her thighs. Naked, she sprawled on the bed.

"You'll see," she said to him, pouting, playful, "I'm not so unlovable. You take me back, you'll have a good time—if you dare!"

He was awake again. Sweetness flooded his being. He felt like a man without a conscience. He actually felt around for Ann.

Not there. Of course. It was an impossible sweetness, full of chocolate and naked symbolism. The real Ann hated him. He didn't feel any too good about her, either. The real wife he loved was Penny.

But the dream said nothing was lost. Access was denied, yes.

That was wisdom. But now he felt the "So near, and yet so far" sensation. No wonder Ann still hated him. He who had known her so lovely, youthful, happy, had removed that image of herself. Dan had stolen years of Ann, locked them up where she couldn't get at them. The same went for him, with her. Dan and Ann would never sit in a room together again and say "Remember when?" They would sculpt, separately. It was parallel play. Mommy and Daddy had left them alone. They were alone, together, them and the rest of the world.

When Dan got home, he looked at his piece about Ann and despaired. Her fault, his fault . . . it was the fault of a society that didn't know what it wanted marriage to be: romantic imbroglio, business deal, kindergarden, buddy-system, duel to the death? Dan had learned that the one chance for a marriage to survive was if both parties abandoned every hope they had had of it, save that it persist.

He melted the piece down. He was left with a bicameral lump the size of two fists and weighing three pounds. Sentimental Ann would have thought it looked like a human heart, and then become disgusted at her own projection. But no heart was that big. Besides, the heart has four chambers, not two. Dan came to see it as a human brain. But Penny said it looked like a petrified piece of cake, inedible but deceptively alluring. And irredeemably lasting, Dan sighed.

Down from the Mountain

Brian and Vera were going to spend a week in the mountains to get away from it all. They had rented a cabin by a creek and brought some detective novels and a deck of cards for the evenings and in the day they hung out by the creek which had a clear pool with a granite bottom and a small sandy beach which got the afternoon sun. The water was bone-chilling and they were glad of the warm sand and the intense high-altitude sun. After a while lying on the blanket they started to sweat. Then they would go back into the pool to cool off.

It was an idyll. This they both knew. They might grow wistful when the time came for them to leave, but neither of them wanted to stay there forever. Their lives were with people and among the necessities of twentieth-century people, the cars and the smog and the hassle of the overcrowded cities. But for a week, they were pleased to be able to put it aside.

On their way back down, they stopped in to see a man, a famous guru, who lived in these mountains. This was something Brian had arranged. He wished that Vera weren't with him for this part of the trip, because she placed less credence in this guru, who went by the name of Theodore Thoroughgood, than did Brian. In fact, when Theodore Thoroughgood had come to the city to address his followers there, and had told of his new house in the mountains that ten neighbors and friends had taken a year to build for T.T. and his family, Vera had piped up and inquired whether this meant that Mr. Thoroughgood would spend the next ten years of his life helping his friends and neighbors build houses. Brian had been mortified by her impertinence, and had made her promise to be on her best behavior during the day at the guru's retreat. Vera had said that she would, but Brian still wished that he were on his own for this leg of the trip.

They parked their car in the clearing in the woods that the map Thoroughgood had sent to them indicated, and gathering their possessions, hiked in the last quarter mile. The trail led through a lovely forest of conifers to a wide clearing. In it stood a beautiful house of open aspect, and there to greet them were Mr. and Mrs. Thoroughgood, together with a number of others. The guru, clad only in a loincloth, greeted them with his amazing smile, which made his smooth face wrinkle (as Vera had said) as if he had just stepped out of Shangri-La into his real age. Brian wished he didn't have to recall this remark of Vera's at such a profound moment. But so gracious was Thoroughgood, who even insisted that Brian and Vera address him as Teddy, that Brian soon put away his chagrin and started to enjoy himself.

The others present were disciples of Teddy's, Teddy said, who were permitted to camp in the woods of Teddy's estate while learning the lore of woodcraft and its underlying principles. A target pinned to some bales of straw, and a bow together with a quiverful of arrows nearby, exemplified the kind of lessons being learned; this was not mere game-playing, they were told, but a means to survival when civilization, with its guns and bullets, should collapse—as it shortly would. All of Theodore Thoroughgood's teaching was based on this premise. It seemed a reasonable one to Brian. In fact, he figured it was collapsing already. The rule of reason had been set aside in favor of a congeries of competing camps, *soi-disant* "philosophies" and lifestyles. Teddy offered something to cling to in these shifting currents.

After Brian had tried his luck with the bow (no one got hurt) they were given a tour of the property. Brian had to agree with Vera that it was a nice piece of real estate. Of water, there was apparently an abundance—a large pond in the middle of the clearing beckoned, for the afternoon was hot, and soon they and the Thoroughgoods were skinny-dipping. It was more than six feet deep, so much was clear, and Teddy told them that he had dug it out himself.

"What a lot of work that must have been," Brian said admiringly.

"Yes, it took me the best part of two days with a tractor and a back-hoe," Thoroughgood replied gravely. Vera began to splutter, but it could be assumed, Brian saw, that she had simply swallowed some water.

Dinner was prepared in a field-kitchen and the good bottle of Sonoma County wine that Brian and Vera had brought to give to their host was quickly consumed. Talk turned to mutual acquaintances. Most of these were men half a generation older than Brian, of an age with Thoroughgood, men Brian's feelings towards were ambivalent. Each in his way had done heroic deeds, but each was given to a macho one-upmanship that Brian felt limited their contribution to the new spirit. Among these was Paul Skald, known as "Heap Big" Skald by some of Brian's irreverent peers, because of his attachment to North American Indian ways, an attachment these peers spoke of as touristic and the outcome of an unacknowledged self-loathing on Skald's part, which caused him to despise his own race. But why not? thought Brian, seeing how whites were hellbent on ruining the planet, acting like lords of creation.

"Paul got tenure at Pepperton U.," Thoroughgood was saying. "That was good news. Another of our team in a position of power."

Brian swallowed. He was afraid Vera would blurt out what he had told her—how, when Skald first got hired at Pepperton, Brian had asked him if it was a tenure-track position, and Skald had snarled back at him that *he* wasn't interested in tenure, that no one could pin a label on Paul Skald, that life was a thing of moment, not of the dull safety of an academic niche. He was afraid that Vera would repeat this now, and add something like maybe Brian should send him a congratulatory telegram. But she stayed silent. However, her eyes sought out his and he looked hastily down.

"Yes," he said at last. "That is good news. Surprisingly good news."

Thoroughgood had hand-rolled a cigaret of some native Indian herbs, and this he proceeded to pass to Brian and Vera, just as if it were a joint. Each inhaled gingerly. When in Rome, Brian found himself saying, to himself of course. When in Shangri-La. When in Sherwood Forest. This reminded him of a joke.

"I want to tell a joke," he said, inserting himself into a gap

122

in Thoroughgood's talking. Brian realized the joke had nothing to do with what Teddy Thoroughgood had been talking about, but it was too late to stop now. Besides, wasn't this to live in the moment, to turn on a dime? "The Sheriff of Nottingham says 'I'm very important at court. No one there can pull strings without Nottingham.' "

Vera giggled briefly, but Teddy Thoroughgood went on as though nothing had happened. Two-thirds of humanity had to die in order for the remaining one-third to live in a decently human fashion. Famine, pollution, wars, starvation: Armageddon was nigh. But those who had had the foresight to head for the hills before the final eve of destruction would survive, would build the new Jerusalem in the ruins of the old, would restore the life-enhancing principles of pre-civilized man. This they owed, these prescient ones, to the human race.

"Dirty work, but somebody's got to do it," Vera observed pleasantly. Teddy continued, apparently deaf to her remark. Brian was looking around for Ruth Thoroughgood. She had hardly said a word to them all day. He wondered what she was like. It must be an awe-inspiring thing to be the wife of a genius. Then he saw her, asleep on a sleeping-bag in the little meadow beside the campfire.

"You brought sleeping-bags, I see," Teddy Thoroughgood said, rising. "That is good. You will unroll them at that side of this little meadow. Ruth and I shall sleep on this side, near to the fire. At six o'clock, I shall rise and wind the conch-shell horn. This will summon the disciples to worship in another meadow half-a-mile from this one. You may sleep another hour. Breakfast will be at the field kitchen at seven. Sleep well." And he gave them for the last time that night his famous leaving-Shangri-La grin.

Brian did not like camping out. The ground was invariably uneven, and hard, and the night dark and foreign. But to sleep in the same small meadow with Theodore—Teddy!—Thoroughgood and his wife was a privilege to make any discomfort worth it. He snuggled down beside Vera and looked at the stars—certainly an amazing sight up here, beyond the smog. He sighed, wishing all the people in San Jose and Los Angeles and San Diego could be here now, studying them.

Vera read his mind, only in her own twisted way.

"Do you buy all that bullshit about L.A. and San Jose having to be wiped out in order for us to survive?" She spoke with some urgency, but kept her voice low.

"Well . . ." Brian began.

"We fly over them every time we go to visit my folks," she went on. "I can't see anyone getting those places back in their box. Besides, my folks live in L.A. And my Aunt Flo is in San Jose. I'd miss them. I don't think I want to live in Teddy's future."

"You always take hold of the stick by the wrong end," Brian snapped, trying to whisper. "Teddy doesn't want to harm your family. He's simply stating that the inevitable is going to happen."

"It's a self-fulfilling prophecy," Vera replied.

Brian tried to recall the exact meaning of the phrase, but his mind felt muzzy. Rather than continue their talk, he regarded the stars once more.

He waited for sleep to come, but it didn't. Of course, he and Vera usually went to bed at one A.M., and it couldn't be later than eleven. But also, the ground was very bumpy. And the night was growing colder. A sound in the underbrush caught his ear. Quickly, he ran through a possible list: raccoon . . . opossum . . . *skunk* . . . fox . . . coyote . . . *wolf* . . . deer . . . *bear!* He had no bow-and-arrow at his side. He began to be afraid of the future: did he have what it took to live in the wilderness?

"Do you hear those noises?" Vera whispered. So she, too, was having a hard time falling asleep.

"Yes," he hissed. "Should we tell Teddy?"

"It's probably just a disciple going to the bathroom," she told him. "Anyway, if we're going to get eaten by a wild animal, I say let's let it happen. That'll be two down, and only five billion to go."

§

Finally, incredibly, a glimmer of light penetrated the glade. Brian had been awake all night. There had been other noises in the bushes, new lumps under his sleeping bag. Quickly the sky brightened. Infinitely weary, Brian turned on his side and fell asleep.

124

To be woken almost at once, he felt, by an odd sound, odder than any he had heard that night. It had sounded somehow out of place. What had it been? But before he had time to consider it further, he saw Teddy Thoroughgood stand up from his sleeping bag with a curious thing in his right hand, which he proceeded to lift to his bearded lips. And then he blew into it—an eerie booming filled the glade. The conch-shell horn! Brian was transfixed by this primal vision, a naked man blowing into an archaic instrument. This sight made the night's sufferings pale into insignificance. It was a sight he would remember always, would tell his children about, should he survive to have any, and should they be born with ears and the ability to fathom language.

He was still full of it when Vera awoke and he tried to tell her something of what he had felt, seeing it. But Vera needed coffee. They dressed, peed in the bushes and stumbled over to the field kitchen. To their surprise, a disciple was already there, stirring something in a big pot hung over the fire. He greeted them amiably.

"How come you aren't at morning service?" Vera queried.

"Teddy excused me," the young man answered. His name, he told them, was Pinecone. "One of us is excused each morning, to prepare breakfast. This is my first time." He peered hopefully into the pot. There wasn't any coffee.

When Teddy Thoroughgood turned up, he checked out the pot and scolded Pinecone.

"Can't you read the directions on the side of the box?"

Pinecone hung his head, devastated.

Brian and Vera thought it was high time they got on the road. They would eat a real breakfast at the first greasy spoon they found on the road. They thanked Teddy for his hospitality, and would have thanked Ruth, too, if they had seen her. Courtly to the end, he walked them some of the way up the trail towards the vehicle station.

"Keep up the good work," Thoroughgood said to them, or perhaps only to Brian. "Together, we will save the world." He gave them an oriental salute before melting into the landscape.

Once in the car, Vera was unstoppable. Brian was going to made to pay for her silence.

"Where does this guy get off?" she screamed, hilarious. "He comes to the city, charges ten bucks a head, takes their money and puts it into his little place in the country. Him and Bobby Bounty!" Vera alluded to a second guru, who often lectured on the same bill with Thoroughgood. "They remind me of the Duke and the Earl, rafting all the way to the bank!"

Brian didn't know which he found more offensive in this speech, the suggestion that Bounty and Thoroughgood resembled deadbeats from Mark Twain, or the implied racial slur—a slant-wise reference to Teddy's orientalism. But he spoke anyway.

"People who try to save the world always get persecuted," he answered icily. "Look at Christ. But of course your people deny Him." He paused, wondering if this constituted a racial slur—it was so hard to tell, these days. He shifted to sounder ground. "Theodore Thoroughgood goes to the Orient for certain wisdoms not available in the decadent and egocentric West. Of course it's all a joke to you. What isn't?"

"My stomach, that's what isn't," Vera replied, almost amicably. Brian sensed that she was willing to soft-pedal things for the present: she had an anecdotal deposit in her Sarcasm Fund that would keep her in the conversational black for weeks.

They stopped at a lunch-counter and ate an all-American breakfast. Brian was quiet, and Vera wanted to know why. She hoped she hadn't been too offensive about his guru.

"I'm trying to remember a sound." And he went ahead and told her about the strange noise that had preceded Thoroughgood's getting up to blow the conch-shell. It had been, he said, gropingly, as he scanned the track of the phenomenon, a strangely mechanical sound, a sort of whirring, muffled sound. Maybe he had dreamed it?

Vera looked at his face, her eyes bright with mischief. "And you still don't know what it was?"

"Of course not, and I don't suppose you do either," he told her.

"It was an alarm-clock, that's what it was! An alarm-clock!"

As soon as Vera uttered the words "alarm-clock" Brian realized she was right. She had hit the nail on the head. Theodore Thoroughgood had needed a piece of mechanical civilization to get his day in the wilderness started. It was an inadmissible picture. He must never give Vera the satisfaction of acknowledging the accuracy of her guess.

"Nonsense," he said, airily. "It was no such thing. Maybe it was a, uh, a rattler. Yes, that's what it must have been, a rattlesnake! I never even thought of that. I'd forgotten all about rattlesnakes."

Vera kept her lips clamped tight shut. They paid the bill and drove on.

Suddenly the car filled with laughter.

"An *alarm*-clock!" Vera was doubled over. "And did you see his jeep? Several hundred expendable humans paid ten bucks a head to buy him that! And what does he run it on? Chickenshit?"

"Prophets have always been subject to ad hominem attacks," Brian sneered. "His arguments are irrefutable. So you attack the man. We're all caught in the contradictions of late capitalism . . ." He went on, with a weary interior sense of bad faith. But nothing could quiet Vera now. Brian saw a creek below a bridge as they drove across, green and chill-looking in the foothill heat. He pulled in and parked.

"Let's swim." They took their towels and wound down the hillside, stripped to their underwear, and went in. Only then, in the eternal chill of the snow-melt water (albeit tainted with lead, selenium and other acidic tailings), did Vera settle down and let her breathing become regular. Her brown eyes flashed in her rosy face and her smile was relaxed, unforced. Brian felt a wave of love pass through him. But the respite, he knew, could only be temporary. They couldn't stay in this mountain creek forever.

Dumb Sven

Where is it Aristotle says we can only know absolute essence through phantasm, sense impression, memory, and maybe words? I *think* I read that in Aristotle. We can't be looking things up all the time. And after all, Aristotle or no Aristotle, we have our lives to lead, and they won't wait for us. Take Sven, for example.

Sven was just a dumb Swede.

He had emigrated to America.

Once here, he had worked hard, and saved a bit of money.

He had fallen in love, and asked the woman to marry him.

She was an American.

Yes, she said. Her name was Kathy.

Dumb Swedes don't grow on trees.

But their ways are not always our ways.

Nor are ours theirs.

Kathy went to the police.

You say you have an intuition that something terrible is about to happen, but you can't tell us what? Don't you mean, you won't tell us what? Well we can't help you if you won't tell us what. I'd suggest you take yourself off to the women's shelter.

Once she was gone, the two officers conferred further. She wouldn't say what, one said. Yeah, said the other, something unspeakable. We'd better stake the place out. Yeah, said the first, But let's not leave it at that. You mean—? the other said. Right, the first replied. This is a job for the Pharaohs. The Pharaohs—a vigilante group composed of insurance salesmen, college instructors, cab drivers, realtors and police. They slipped out of their uniforms and into their striped cars.

When Kathy got to the women's shelter they told her she couldn't stay there unless she had been battered. So she said that she had been battered. She hadn't anywhere else to stay. So the woman she had spoken to told Kathy she could stay there. And she tried to get Kathy to tell her everything she knew concerning Sven's past. But Kathy still loved Sven and so she didn't say much. Something unspeakable, huh? said the woman who had interviewed her. And she went off to confer with others of her dynamic sisterhood. We'll fix the sonofabitch's little red wagon, they agreed. Kathy was so defenseless, so despicably feminine, so—appealing. The women slipped into their VW buses.

And the one who was also a member of a low-to-the-ground religious sect took her story to the next meeting of the More-of-us-than-thousian society, who take it upon themselves to correct those suspected of unspeakable sins. They drive vans painted white with dark curtains across the windows.

When Sven told a colleague at work that Kathy had disappeared, and that he was being followed by white Dodge vans and VW buses and green cars with racing stripes down the side, and that his house was being staked out by the police, and that he feared Kathy had been kidnapped, this colleague went straight to the director. The director was the head of a rather large organization, and believed in curing wayward employees by, for instance, planting cocaine in their desks and changing the locks. He had joined the organization after Sven and wanted Sven out so that a friend of his could be brought in to fill Sven's position. He agreed with the colleague, who knew of the director's animosity toward Sven, and wanted the man's approval so that he could obtain a promotion, that Sven was on the edge and should be given a light shove over. He might never come back. So the colleague took to phoning Sven evenings and hanging up when Sven answered. Meanwhile Sven's director had one of his private male secretaries follow Sven in a souped-up Porsche. One evening it passed Sven at 90 on a lonely country road, and then slowed down.

Sven did a U-turn and drove straight to the mental hospital. He was followed there variously by a white Dodge van, a blue VW bus, a striped Mustang, a Sheriff's car, and the FBI, who kept a file on the More-of-us-than-thousians, driving another white Dodge van, and the more usual telephone-repair truck. Each of these did a U-turn in the parking lot of the hospital as Sven staggered into that sanctuary.

He was given a large pill to blur his perceptions and a room to share with a man who may have been saying the Mafia wanted 25 grand to release Kathy without further harm. When Sven, after 3 days of this, complained to the ward-charge, that functionary took him into a room, locked the door, and told Sven that he, Sven, was in the power of witches, that evidence was being planted in his house that would send him to the pen for 25 years, that his house had been wired for sound, and that Sven had two alternatives: the back wards, where he would be killed sooner or later by another patient at the order of the witches, or to go home, where he would also be killed, sooner or later. At this moment, they were interrupted by a phone call for Sven. It was Kathy. He could tell from her voice she was under duress. And how did she know where to find him? And why did she tell him he was in a bind? After he hung up, the ward-charge warned Sven that the last patient who had known so much about his persecutors, had had to be dealt with immediately. At a certain point, the human ability to cope with reality becomes impaired. But Sven had now passed that point. He decided to lie.

When the psychiatrist saw him the next day, Sven told him: I do not believe that police cars, white Dodge vans with dark curtains drawn across the windows, VW buses with pussy power bumper stickers, Mustangs with stripes on them, or a souped-up Porsche have been following me, watching my house, or that persons driving any of the above have broken into my house to plant evidence against me, or that my wife has been kidnapped and is being held for ransom, or that the ward-charge Sterling Steeringstrait is an agent of the devil and representative of a coven of witches dedicated to the destruction of my immortal soul.

Very good, the doctor murmured. Have another pill. And soon Sven was allowed to go home.

To his surprise, delight and terror, Kathy was waiting there for him. Did the gang send you? Sven wanted to know. Don't start that stuff again, she told him, You just about broke my heart with that rap when I called you at the hospital. They told me you were cured.

Sven had forgotten to lie. Such was the power of his love for Kathy. He quickly corrected himself. You are not a witch, he told her, nor by your actions did you cause me to be followed by VW buses, white Dodge vans, Porsches, striped Mustangs with men with mikes held up to their mouths, who did U-turns in front of our house when I parked and came in, but wait till I tell you what this ward-charge said to me! And when he had finished, Kathy thought, quien sabe? and said to Sven: There are evil persons in this world. When you are down, they will try to hurt you. But that doesn't add up to a plot.

And she took him out into the main street of town on Friday night and made him watch the parade of cars and sure enough, within an hour at least one of each—white Dodge van, VW bus, striped Mustang, Porsche with dealer's plates, police car, telephone-repair truck, and the same kind of VW bug that Sterling Steeringstrait always drove—had gone by. There are cars everywhere, Sven, Kathy told him. This is America. More than that, this is California. Sven, she went on, I realized, while we were apart, that I misjudged you. It's simply that I'm American and you're not. Let's help one another to understand better. I would like that very much, Sven replied. Particularly I would like to understand this great country of yours.

And so each night, Kathy would watch the TV news with Sven, and explain it to him, and each morning, she would read the morning paper with him, and explain that. Sven heard about wives being kidnapped for ransom, religious sects persecuting innocent individuals, patients in mental hospitals being driven to suicide, secret organizations within the forces of law and order who took both into their own hands, men being harassed by feminist groups (oh!—deservedly), employees being set up by their employers, workers being betrayed by their colleagues, husbands being duped by their wives. And he learned to repeat the prayer Kathy taught him: I am not that important. I am not that important.

The trouble is, Sven said to me, when he told me all this, I keep adding a line to that prayer. What is it? I wanted to know. Sven said: I could be mistaken for anyone else.

I wish he hadn't added that part. If I'm killed in an

131

intersection collision, I want to go out thinking it's an accident.

I want to die confirmed in my imagination of the way things really are.

Despicable People

May was right. June and Ace hadn't gone thru it yet. So this was what she had been going thru with Timmy, all that time Ace was bewildered and baffled at the obstacles she was putting in the way of their happiness. And for his own part, he hadn't even known that he was bringing his portion of misery into the apartment.

When he would see her, June was doing just fine, thank you, she might throw in an "I hate you, you creep" but she was in control. She was Miss Control of 1965, forever. Ace sighed relief. He had known he could count on her—that she had read this kind of situation through, in novels. And so Ace had gotten off scot-free, a new love in his arms, a bit of guilt that could loom large enough between 3 and 6 A.M., when God is off-duty and has his pre-recorded tape hooked up to his Absolute Telephone, but nothing he couldn't handle. And soon enough, June's news was all of this stud, Hungdog, and the camping trip he had taken her on, just like that, on the spur of the moment, the way Ace never did anything anymore, if you overlooked his leaving her, and they had gone far up, high into the mountains, and bathed in the mountain streams, and done it under the stars, and Ace was very, very relieved to listen to these details. It wasn't until much later that it occurred to him he was meant to be very, very jealous.

Because he wasn't. But as the weeks grew into months, and May turned hot and cold in his arms, and didn't tell him it was because her conscience was doing it to her with Timmy, Ace grew appalled. He had blown it. He had given up his lovely home and gardens, his daughter, who in truth was inseparably dear to him, and the most sensible wife a man could hope to know, and a lot of fun too. He was stuck in a dreary city apartment with a girl who didn't know her own mind and wouldn't let him discover it, and only one fact to keep him there: he was in love with her. But any fool knows love comes then goes, leaving the fool stranded, his worldly good crisped on the altar of Vain Hopes. And about this time June grew softer to him when they would meet in the hallways of the place they fortuitously both worked at. How was her life? Oh ho-hum, doin ok, got a lodger to help with the rent, finishing her novel about her and Ace, by the way would he write her a check to help with the house payments, and apart from that, well, now she had it all in perspective she could see it was a Good Thing Ace had left her. In fact she could see it was actually that she had gotten him to leave. She had been getting stronger all these years and he had been getting, well, not weaker, but a bit of a drag. He was still dropping cigaret ash on the rugs long after she June had quit smoking because of her terrible bronchitis which it was too bad he Ace hadn't contracted also. So she had kicked him out and finally, getting her message, he had found some pretty young thing to flatter him and Bob's your uncle. It was Karma. Now Ace had to do the cooking and the driving and the banking which he had used to push onto June and serve him right but she didn't put it that way, Karma was the word for such Cosmic Justice.

All of this Ace agreed to, delighted to be off the hook so lightly. And he heard from his daughter who had gone (as anyway had for years been understood about this time she would have done) to live with her mother, June's precursor, in Runcible Junction, that the kid was settling in ok. So: now, if only May would stop backing off, they would be in Clear City for good. But May backed away. No, it wasn't Timmy, she was thru with him, though true she hadn't been as thru with him when she started falling in love with Ace as she had let Ace think; but no, she was over that one, just that her parents and Timmy kept trying to get her to feel guilty about it. And so she was going to move to her own apartment until the divorces came thru. It was the only way for a decent Catholic girl to go. Ace understood, didn't he? He loved her, so he must. He wasn't to interpret her moving out as rejection.

But somehow, he couldn't help himself. He did. After all, he had elected long since, hardly without knowing it, to give falling in love all the respectful distance it deserved. He knew it led

134

to one party or the other trying to strand the other on the jetty the way that bitch had stranded that sincere, handsome guy in Lina Wertmuller's fine movie, *Swept Away*. He had let himself be swept away and now here was May, sweeping him under the rug. May was going to ditch him for Timmy, parents, and the Church. And besides, good sense, since if she was May, he was October. By the time he was 121 she would be only 100. It wasn't that she didn't love him, but on the contrary, that she loved him so much it scared her. So instead of running away there was this apartment just down the street and he could find her there any time, or maybe almost any time, he desired. There. Now everyone would be happy. May, anyway.

As he slowly turned this way or that on the stake he had been hung on out here where the winds of the world blow, Ace recalled June's renewed pleasantness in his presence, how when he looked into her eyes the evening of that day May had put him thru another of her baffling and grief-stricken silences, he had glimpsed once more the understanding and reciprocity that 12 years can hardly help but make available to a separated couple feeling themselves each and each down on their romantic luck. And he recalled too how June had never put him thru it the way May could. He had never been in love with June the way he was with May. He hadn't needed to be. June had adjusted to him with her own version of being in love and he had seen only what he had been shown: good company, loyalty, great stepmother to the kid. He had enjoyed great contentment, peace, security, and some happiness; presumably June had too, as their marriage went on and on and all those about them were losing theirs. True, June, when now they would meet, would assure him there'd been an underside: how she had done all the housework, laundry, etc., while he had been working full-time; how she had, for fear of his anger, taken great care to give him no cause for suspicion. He agreed, glad to hear her speak to his guilt, and gave little thought to the element of choice she'd had in all of these decisions. At this point May had left him with one last slam of the passenger door and June's spiel was sweetness and light in Ace's ears. Here at least was someone who understood him. She was looking good.

One time when he and May knew they had irrevocably parted he fled to his old home and June took him in. He was back! They would have a big new year's party to announce the happy fact. Lunch of course would have to be told. Lunch was the lodger and now for the first time it dawned on Ace, also June's live-in lover. What will Lunch make of this? he queried. June didn't seem to be bothered at all. Possibly there were sensible arrangements for loving to be had in this world, and June and Lunch had one, Ace thought. But he left next day.

Why? Still in love with May, that's why. Though by now he could see this was one of those relationships bent on keeping the other alive in order to go on killing them. And that he was one of those despicably neurotic creatures bent on his own destruction. All he wanted was to be with May again, look into her sweet face, and feel himself alive. Until she left him again. And then again. He realized he might have something to do with these leavings, but he didn't think so. If May didn't know he loved her by now, after all the shit she'd put him thru and here he still was coming after her, then maybe one more reconciliation would prove it. Each time she left he went straight to hell. Words baffle description. Hope keeps on springing. He was a dead duck. It was unbearable. He would be thru with May before she had wrung the last ounce of submission out of him, by God. He would examine the rubble and build, bit by careful bit, a little temple of life once more, for him to live in. He called June. Yes, she'd be delighted to spend the weekend with him. Lunch would be away anyway. See you soon. Ace had to realize he had been mistaken. At forty-five you don't ruin your carefully built up life for love. Uh, that is, for male menopausal passion, vain attempt to nail youth to the floor. Yes, it was strange being with June again this way, but that was because he had spent so much time with May. And when May came around, after June had returned to his house and Lunch, and he held her tight thru the night once more, he knew it was a big mistake. It would ache that much more next time she ditched him. He began to feel truly insane.

And when he found out that May, each time he spent time with June, was spending time with Timmy, he knew he was doing the right thing. May had lied to him all along! Now he recalled

136

her coming home drunk with her hair coming unpinned after an evening on the town with Timmy ostensibly to tell him how happy she was with Ace and to try to get Timmy to be no more than her friend. It had all been hysterical denial. What was love, anyway? Surely it would yield to analysis. Being in love is an unhealthy regressive neurotic dependency, give me a Pal, some peace of mind and a place to think in, the rest is bullshit. And June wanted to be his pal, as ever. It would be hard, but he'd break with May. Heal himself. Learn to love June as before. If she'd let him.

Sure, she'd let him. Nothing easier. Take him back into their house. She'd tell Lunch she didn't want him as a lover anymore. He was welcome to go on living upstairs and be friends. Never mind, as she told Ace, that sometimes, holding on to Lunch in the night, she'd felt maybe she loved the guy. Lunch wasn't really and truly the man for her. It had been him, Ace, all down the line, and never mention Hungdog, Lunch, Carl Gustav Dong, or any other of the instruments of June's loneliness and need to make Ace jealous. She wanted it all, and would ditch anyone without hesitation in the gamble to get it. She had free will and so she chose.

Lunch, also, had freedom to choose and gave his notice. Fine, let him, Ronnie from down the road was breaking up with his wife and wanted to move in. How neatly the pieces were falling into place! Ace thought of a movie he had once seen, of a broken glass played backwards reconstituting itself, but feeling himself no more than one of the pieces, kept it to himself. It was great to be home. He paced the neglected gardens, assuring himself that at some point his head would stop delivering him these incessant pictures of May. He offered friendship to Lunch, feeling no jealousy towards the man. This too, would be a matter of reproach from June, proof that he wasn't in love with her. But when she told him Lunch disliked him, he saw that June had treated Lunch badly. It was hardly Ace Lunch disliked, since he had exchanged only a dozen words with him all week. It was the situation, to which June, in her selfishness, turned a reasonably blind eye. June couldn't see beyond her own need to be happy. And no more could Ace, as he tried to put May out of his mind and refocus on June.

But when he did, he grew alarmed. He began to believe that June had been right, back when she had assured him she was the first to know she and he were all washed up. Over their years together, she had developed, without his being aware of it, this habit of answering the questions she put to him before he had time to consider her words. She always had this picture of whatever she was in, and this picture supplied her with questions the answers whereto she already, grace of her picture, knew. Lacking a picture himself, he felt Socratized, over and over. But he realized that, the longer the pause before he himself answered, the greater June's fear grew that he was cooking up a lie, and thus her panic supplied the answer she most feared, filling his mouth with words he could neither swallow nor reject, such were her over-simplifications of what, seeing it was his life, he felt to be complex beyond what her maneuvers could describe. And in short, even had his head not been available to memories of May, he had no business here. It was cruel, that by ceasing to love one's wife, one lost one's house and grounds, but as his friend Zenny Rollins pointed out, it happened all the time. It was all very well for June to assure him she no longer ever again believe me! wanted a dependent relation with him. That they would do it a day at a time. Her actions proved the impossibility of this proclaimed ideal. Each day delivered him testimony to the wrongheadedness of this hope. God knew Ace admired the woman and wanted her friendship till kingdom come, but the next time she treated him like a not-too-bright student was, suddenly, the last: if he waited another day, she would think herself that much further back in the saddle and riding her favorite burro, flattered to have such a handsome and well-thought-of mount. So he bucked.

So May had been right, and too bad, since she'd known this from the word Go almost, that she had been unable to get Ace to see what she knew; that she had told him this only yesterday, by letter. But at least she had told him. That he and June had never really gone thru the wretchedness of divorce, the way May had been going thru it with Timmy all these months. Well, now here was the shit, with the fan working. When Ace told June he couldn't be her lover, that he had reached the end of his ability to try, you might have supposed the woman would be speechless.

Au contraire, as they used to say in the Age of Reason, beloved by June in fantasy: She would ruin him; she would kill herself; she would never love again; how dare he talk to her about May when she kept asking him to talk about her; he was a creep and a shit, as May well knew also; he would get exactly what he deserved; he would be happy with his love while for her, June, life was over; he was a despicable corruption of the human, capable of nothing but flip-flop-flip; all this Ace recognized, since he had been thru this pain whenever May walked out on him. June really did love him. But he really loved May. And seeing they each really loved, what were these charges they so readily leveled against the object of their love, what were these reasons each paraded, as if love were thus available to a lesser power? Why couldn't June admit she and Ace were in that boat together, anyway? I was doing fine until you walked back into my life, said June, but hadn't she invited him back in, trampling on Lunch's feelings in the process?

But now Ace was trying to reason with love, too. He had to let June go, and she, him, and it had taken a year to reach this moment. It was ghastly. It was why they had delayed the confrontation. It was why May had backed away, why June had refused to love Hungdog and Lunch, why she had encouraged Ace to think of them in such terms as supplied these trivializing names for two poor suffering mortals, it was the lightning flash that rove the house in twain, finally. Maybe Ace had left it too late to tell May what he had found out about this life's priorities. At least he could now go into whatever came next knowing there was nothing to trust but love; knowing that June was feeling that of all powers, love was the least to be trusted at all. And to that double-bind, Ace believed he could tell only one fact, the feeling that in the present moment overwhelmed him. It was not the morality which had raised him—like hell it wasn't! Superior persons would need to refer to the particular hole in which their particular ace lay. But what made it all so painful was the far-from-blunt saw that the feelings we have for someone can never equal that someone. He never wanted to acknowledge this other fact, of which he stayed therefore barely half-aware. And so despite, that masks our fear—the fear Ace had of his own unconscious—

got projected outwards upon these threatening figures, threatening to him because he wanted to place his emotional life in their hands. And June was no better. About May, however, though the youngest of them all, could be discerned a rare objectivity. That was what kept her back-pedalling, Ace saw, and therefore, what kept him in pursuit.

Sven's Cadillac

Sven and Kathy's friends and associates all drove automobiles made in Japan, but Sven and Kathy were too poor for that, so they had to drive American cars. If they could have afforded the initial outlay, they would have saved money on gas mileage and repairs, for this is the way in which the rich get richer and the poor poorer as decreed by the morality of our society. But Sven and Kathy were too poor to buy their cars unused, and so they were always having to fork over for repairs. But what were they to do? Exiguous as their salaries were, they had to get to their jobs, and their jobs, as prescribed by society, were a stiff drive from where they could afford to live. This was to keep the petroleum companies happy.

Sven being a poor immigrant lad had the ambition to own a Cadillac. Currently he drove a Chevy Nova. It was a '75, made back when Chevys still resembled American cars, and because of that, and because the letters on its license plate were NML, Kathy referred to it as "Mr. Normal." It was indeed a most normal-looking vehicle, suitable to a recent immigrant trying to look more American. But now it was 1985, and Mr. Normal was starting to have problems. It was like having an aging pet that has to be taken to the vet every month or so. You have to make hard decisions: its life versus your pocket-book.

Luckily for Sven, the decision was taken out of his hands. One night in a fierce rainstorm he drove three blocks to the local videostore and when he came back out he couldn't find his car. There was one that resembled it slightly, with a young man standing next to it in the driving rain scribbling on a piece of paper. A large white pickup was sloppily double-parked in front of this now oddly familiar car which was, Sven realized with a rush of alarm and anger, Mr. Normal with a huge dent in the driver's side.

He was a very decent young man, who could have kept going after he had skidded into Sven's parked car but had instead stopped to write a note about how to contact him. So there was nothing to worry about, the damage would be paid for, and Mr. Normal would soon be as good as new—well, as good as he had been before Sven left him unattended for five minutes so that he could rent *The Devil Thumbs a Ride.* Yes, to Sven, Mr. Normal had a life of his own, Sven had endowed this piece of machinery with quasi-human qualities, and in this sense was no more civilized than some South Seas cargo-culter. So he was very relieved to learn that his car would soon be as right as rain again.

So he was all the more desolated after his insurance representative came to visit and told him his car was a total wreck because to fix it would cost more than the book said it was worth and Sven would only be paid $800 take it or leave it, which he could apply towards the cost of repair or towards the purchase of another car if he wanted to junk this one. Junk Mr. Normal! Put Sven's pet to sleep! Possibly the insurance man worked for the opposition, or Sven had misunderstood something he said. Sven still had a few things to learn about America. But when Sven called his own company, they confirmed what he had been told.

When Sven took his outrage and indignation to Kathy, she cleverly deflected both. She pointed out that he had had Mr. Normal for seven years now, and that the average American, such as Sven wanted to become, changed cars every four years. And knowing of Sven's secret ambition she told him about an office-mate of hers who had a Cadillac to sell. Why not ask the price and if it was right give it a test drive?

The woman was very nice, Sven thought. She confessed to having a soft spot in her heart for Cadillacs. A shiny recent model stood in her driveway; the somewhat tarnished '72 Coupe de Ville was parked on the street. The woman was delighted when it started right up. She hadn't driven it for a while, she said. There was an odor to its interior that Sven found attractive, a blend of vinyl and burnt oil, but he didn't know it was so constituted. Sven drove around town for a while—himself, Sven Lindstrom, driving around Santa Linda, California, in a Cadillac Coupe de Ville!—and then took it to his mechanic's to get it checked out.

142

His regular mechanic wasn't there, but the two who were said that for $25 they would look at it. He left it there and returned a couple of hours later and they told him it was fine—in fact one of them wrote "OK to buy" on his receipt—so Sven drove back to the woman's house and wrote a check for $1000 then and there, and received in exchange the pink slip and the registration and all of the worksheets that the woman could find. In bliss, he drove his Caddy home to show it to Kathy.

Privately, Kathy thought the faded green an ugly color, but that much car in good working order for $1000 looked like a good deal. And she could see that it cheered Sven up. Soon he would stop mourning Mr. Normal, who had been sold for $200 to some fellows who figured they could use his parts—a kind of organ transplant, Kathy pointed out to Sven, that would give Mr. Normal a sort of immortality.

Two weeks later, with a couple of days off from work so that he didn't need the car, Sven took it in for a tune-up. The mechanics who had checked it out had advised Sven to do this. This time, Sven's regular mechanic was there. Next day, this man had grim news.

"Your number five cylinder's sucking oil."

"Please?"

"You're looking at $1500, $2000."

"But your fellows checked it out okay to buy."

"I don't know anything about that. Got the work order?" Sven showed it to him.

"Let me speak to those guys about this. Meanwhile, don't drive this car. Except straight home."

Dolorously, Sven drove the three blocks. He broke the news to Kathy. Together, they started looking for something Sven could get to the job and back in.

§

Years passed. Sven had another car: a '78 Mercury Grand Marquis, a car even larger than the Caddy. It got about 10 miles to the gallon. This made it politically incorrect. But Kathy's brother, who sold used cars, had gotten them a real deal on it. The Caddy

143

sat in the garage of Sven and Kathy's new house. Nothing had been done to it. It sat there deteriorating. Sven had wanted to take somebody to Small Claims Court about it, but Kathy didn't want him suing her workmate. In all fairness, Sven didn't want to sue her either. When he had gone back to see her, after the shocking news, she had searched further and come up with the work order dated about 6 months before Sven had bought the car, and sure enough, her mechanic had found something amiss with number 5 cylinder. The woman was genuinely distressed that she had neglected to mention this to Sven. Somehow, she didn't know how, she had forgotten about it. It had gone clean out of her head.

But when Sven suggested that he give the car back to her and she return his check to him, she smiled sadly and said that wasn't possible. She and her husband, the attorney, had already used that money to pay off debts.

When Sven told Kathy this, she could hear anger in his voice.

"Those are the breaks, Sven," she told him. "So we lost a thousand dollars. It's part of the price of living in this society. It's still the greatest society in the world."

But Sven thought that any society that permitted such injustice had no claim to be called great.

Then Kathy left that job and took another one, and that cleared the way for Sven to sue. He had called several attorneys who offered a first consultation for free, and received various advice from them. The consensus was that he should sue both the seller and the garage. The time-limit as appointed by statute was fast approaching. Sven wrote letters to the sellers and to the garage-owners detailing his complaint and requesting restitution. He heard from neither party. Now he had to serve them with papers.

It cost $30 to have someone served with these papers. Sven had to serve four people: both owners of the garage, and both wife and husband. That came to $120. That was the price for a professional process-server. These costs would be returned to him if he won his case. He was told that he *could* send these papers by certified mail, but that usually this proved ineffectual, as the persons being served refused to sign for the letter. Sven, while convinced of the justice of his cause, was not so sure of winning

144

in court. He had been two years longer in America at this point.

Then he remembered his friend Bob. Bob was unemployed and short of money. Why not offer Bob $60 to serve the four sets of papers? Bob liked the idea. Sven picked him up and they drove to the garage. The owners, one of whom was Sven's ex-regular mechanic, were both out on calls. Sven and Bob sat in the Grand Marquis listening to the radio. Eventually, Sven went back to inquire again. Neither would be back that day. So Sven picked Bob up again next morning, and they found both men at work and Bob handed them the papers. It was a snap. Sven could have handed them the papers with equal ease. But the court didn't trust him to be telling the truth about that, later. Sven could see the reason for this rule. But still, it irked him. He took comfort in the thought that he was helping his friend out. Next, they had to serve the couple who had sold him the Caddy. They timed their arrival to coincide with the hour most Americans get home from work, before they go out for their busy evenings. The woman seemed delighted to see Sven at her door, and invited him in. There was her husband. Bob came in too, and Sven introduced him, adding that Bob was there to serve them papers concerning the Caddy.

"For Heaven's sake! Is that old thing still kicking around?" The lady of the house couldn't conceal her displeasure. All business, her husband strode forward to receive and inspect his papers. He, too, looked unpleasantly surprised.

"I wrote you a letter," Sven reminded them. "You didn't bother to answer. I was advised that this should be my next step. I'm sorry." Then he and his accomplice left.

The court date rolled around and Sven and Kathy went to the courtroom and waited for their case to be called. Sven stood in front of the judge and spoke his piece. Kathy stood next to Sven and confirmed their version when asked to. They were asking $1500—the estimated cost of repairing the Caddy, plus the cost of serving the papers. One of the garage-owners was there, and he admitted, graciously, Sven thought, that there had been a lapse in procedures and he reckoned his firm was at fault.

Then the husband of the couple who had sold Sven and Kathy the Caddy was called. The judge and he were on a first-name basis.

145

This didn't worry Sven, though, because he could see that the judge was a very fair man. And he was sure, too, that the husband, being an attorney, would be eager to see justice done. And so he was. There was no lemon-law, he reminded the judge, that applied to transactions between individuals. The lemon-law only applied to dealerships. So that the lemon-law could not be invoked in this case. True, he and his wife had neglected to inform Sven that there was a pre-existing condition that would take some costly fixing. But it had been an honest neglect. There had been no intent to deceive. Yet he had been hauled into court to face the implication that he had been less than straightforward in his dealings. He sounded highly indignant. He gestured vehemently towards Sven, who stood only a couple of feet away. Sven realized he had done something shameful, that his actions had somehow suggested that this man had deliberately sold him a lemon. He hastened to explain that he never for one moment had thought it was deliberate. It was simply that there had been something wrong with the car when he had bought it, and he thought that the sellers, when they realized this, would be anxious to return his check and to take the car back.

This only made the husband more indignant. He repeated that the lemon-law didn't apply in this case.

"You mean," Sven asked, "that what would be a sort of crime if committed by a company, is nothing of the kind if committed by an individual?"

The judge said that Sven was using the wrong language, but that it was obvious he came from someplace else, but that even though he was putting it the wrong way, he was essentially correct. He had no case against the sellers but he might have against the garage and now he could step down. He would hear from the court in a couple of weeks.

In a couple of weeks Sven learned that he had won a judgement against the garage, which the court was ordering to do $1400 worth of work on his car. So now the question had become, how to get the car to the garage, which was in the next town. Sven went into his own garage to look at his Caddy. He hadn't been able to bear the sight of it and hadn't looked at it for years. If he had to go into the garage to get a tool he needed, he had somehow blotted the Caddy out of the picture. This hadn't been easy, because it took up more than half the garage, but Sven had not been raised to do only what was easy. Now, to his horror, he saw that some fluid had leaked from the car and was all over the garage floor.

So the next time Kathy's brother Greg came to see them, they took him down into their garage to look at the Caddy. Greg knew about cars.

"Looks like the seals on the transmission have gone," he told them. And he began to explain to them how to go about trying to repair the damage. But then he looked at their faces and decided to change direction. They didn't seem to have taken in anything of what he'd been saying—how the seals dried up in all probability in the summer heat, cracked and let the transmission fluid leak out; how they might try getting fresh seals and simply refilling the transmission. . . . "Look," he resumed, "there's only so many things you can do with a Nehru jacket. Offer the garage half just to forget it. My father-in-law collects Caddies. I'll get him down here to work on it. He'll take it off your hands."

So Sven did this. And sure enough, the garage-owners were pleased to accept the suggestion. Sven actually suggested $100 less than half, in case they wanted to bargain, but they didn't. And in a couple of days, a check for $800 was in the mail. At this point Sven and Kathy were only some $200 out of pocket on the deal—unless time and anxiety could be priced. But when Sven went to the DMV to straighten out the registration and to make sure the Caddy was legally driveable, the clerk noticed the change of address.

"How did you get it from this address to this new one?"

"I drove it."

"But according to these dates, the registration had already lapsed. You could have gotten a special one-day permit to move it. Did you?"

"No, I am very sorry, but I didn't know about that," Sven laughed, smiling winsomely.

But it did him no good. He had to pay $120, which included a kind of fine for being ignorant of the law. So now he was more than $300 out of pocket. He complained to Kathy.

"Listen to me, Sven Lindstrom," she said, firmly. "It costs money to learn things. Oh, you probably can go to college for free in dear old Sweden, but it costs a bundle to go here. Stop your whining! You left Sweden, didn't you? You chose to come here, right? Look, for a mere 300-odd bucks, you've learned how Small Claims Court works, you've learned to be double careful when getting a car checked out, you've learned other stuff besides—transmission seals, and I don't know what-all—and you got to own a Cadillac and even drive it around town a couple of times. Sven," she went on, warming to her mission, "you've said yourself, Sweden is headed for disaster, you can't run a welfare state in a free enterprise world, it's going to crack up and even Poland will have a higher standard of living but you were brought up that way and I know it's hard to change. Be grateful for what you've learned. And thank God that piece of junk is going to be out of our garage one day soon. I want to fix that place up and put my potted plants in there."

Then sure enough, one day her brother Greg and Greg's father-in-law came to town, and spent a day tinkering in the garage, and paid Kathy with a one-dollar bill, and the Caddy was driven away. Sven stood and watched it disappear down the street. The muffler sounded shot, and the drab green paint was chipped and rusting.

"Good riddance," Kathy said, putting her arm round his shoulder.

§

That Christmas, Sven and Kathy drove to the city her brother lived in, to celebrate the holiday with Greg and his wife and their kids. Greg had rented a video-camera for the day and took Sven outside to show him how it worked. Then a classy-looking car drove up—a Caddy, gleaming white. Greg's father-in-law leaned out to wish them Merry Christmas. Then he drove off. Sven felt a wave of envy and resentment rush through his chest. If only he had been more persistent, taken the time to understand what Greg was saying, *he* could have been driving that!

He had omitted to switch the camera off, so naturally, when

148

the day's rushes were shown to the assembled guests after dinner, there was Sven's Caddy, gleaming white and good as new. There were Oohs and Aahs from the guests. Sven ground his teeth. Then someone said, "What's that car in the background? A '78 Mercury? That was a great car, that Grand Marquis model!" It was a woman's voice, low and sexy. Later, Sven realized it had been Kathy's. But she had disguised it well enough at the time.

Sven Makes Friends at Traffic School

Now Sven had to go to traffic-school. He had been driving along one morning, minding his own business, when he had seen a black-and-white in his rear-view mirror. It came up quite close behind him and he thought he recognized the driver as someone who had followed him in a striped mustang during the period of his persecution at the hands of the Pharaohs, a secret law-n-order group that contained not a few policemen among its zealot ranks. At the time of his persecution, Sven had been passed by police-cruisers whose lights would suddenly flash on and then as suddenly stop flashing. Patrol cars shadowed him from one end of Santa Linda to the other. A CHP officer talking to a waitress in a roadside cafe had liberally sprinkled his chat with references to the "two-legged chicken" he was waiting on, waiting for this coward to get back on the road where he could be nabbed.

Yes, in his dark-glasses and uniform cap, this fellow following Sven could well have been any number of his former persecutors. Watching him, Sven knew the worst as the red and blue lights began to blink and revolve. He pulled over. He wound down his window. He learned that he had just run a stop sign. He had been so preoccupied with the view from his mirror that he had failed to notice the sign.

He had not been to traffic school during the last three years, so Sven could go now. It was that or pay $67 and lose a point on his insurance.

Sven signed up at the local junior college. They had courses in everything. They had courses in welding and creative writing and even Swedish, and they had a traffic school course for those who were getting rusty on their rules of the road. To Sven, this latter category seemed to contain just about everyone he saw as he drove along—old men with extra cartilage in their ears who did 37 mph in 55 mph zones, young guys with bushy back hair poking out from under their baseball caps who zipped out from sideroads without coming to a complete halt and counting 1001, 1002, 1003, women deep in conversation with other women who hung lefts in cars that apparently had never had turn-signals installed, slick-looking dudes with car phones to their faces whose gleaming Jags whizzed past Sven at 85 on the freeway, funky dudes hauling trash or roof-tarring machines or tractors who never pulled over to the shoulder but kept on steadily accumulating a convoy behind them, drivers of strangely low-slung cars who were in no hurry to get anywhere and found it amusing that the fanatics behind them might be, women putting on their makeup at 55 mph, men reading the newspaper at 60, and the occasional child, Sven was sure, guiding four tons of metal and 30 gallons of high explosive swiftly down the road to nowhere.

Yes, as Kathy pointed out to him when he mentioned these and other entertainments met along life's way, she and Sven should count themselves fortunate that they hadn't been in serious accidents and maimed or killed, knock on wood, by any of the space-cases and air-heads who had somehow persuaded the DMV to issue them with a license. But now Sven was going to go to traffic school and meet some of these pervert freak delinquents. Better there than in the tank!

Eight hours straight, his friend John Greenleaf had told him, would kill any brain cells Sven had extant, so Sven had signed up to do two nights of four hours each. He was warned to arrive on time, and so he did, taking the one remaining seat in the back row and looking around for beautiful women in mini-skirts or halter-tops. But it was February. The women somehow looked like more men. He had noticed this a lot of late. Perhaps it was his diet. Sharp at six the instructor locked the door and began to address them.

To his dismay, Sven realized the man had a speech impediment. He would be listening to this for eight hours over the next two days. He wondered if this had been cunningly devised as a further punishment by the DMV or whoever ultimately was responsible or whether he should take the charitable view and be glad that the handicapped were being hired. He thought the man said that they should take notes, but possibly he had said the opposite. His hands froze in the air above his notepad. A doodle went unfinished.

The seats were uncomfortable, but they should not try to ease the pain by putting their feet up on the seats in front of them, the instructor said, because the fire-marshal had objected to this practice already. Sven could see the reason for this—it would take almost a second longer to clear the rows between the seats in the event of a fire or other disaster requiring people to exit quickly. Sven approved. It was an orderly way to do things. He began to warm to the instructor.

Looking around again, Sven identified three people who belonged to the Pharaohs, and one FBI agent. He wondered who they were after, this time. Perhaps the instructor himself? Possibly the FBI man was here to check up on the Pharaohs. Or vice versa. Anyway, he himself was safely out of it, he thought smugly. His wife had shown him the futility of being paranoid in a paranoidgenic society.

His eye did light upon one man with whom Sven felt it might be interesting to talk. He was dark and balding, a few years older than himself, and was scribbling away on a notepad. Sven thought this particularly daring, if the instructor had requested that nobody take notes. Sven wondered what else there was about this individual that attracted his attention, and decided it was something about the eyes. Even in profile, they looked haunted—haunted, but not defeated. It was a curious combination.

The instructor was drawn to the anecdote. Now he was speaking of someone who had driven a car across a railroad track just as the train was coming along. The car had been sliced in two. The driver had been only slightly injured. However, he turned out to be drawing 100% disability on the grounds that he was legally blind. Further investigation turned up 7 other licensed drivers in the state who were equally blind. People laughed at this.

Sven wasn't a bit surprised. That he or she was legally or even illegally blind was an explanation that often presented itself to Sven as the only one possible for some of the drivers he encountered on the highways and byways. He was pleased to have this official confirmation of what he had long suspected and indeed alleged, often directly to the offending driver. But he was surprised when the man on his right nudged him and said something Sven couldn't quite catch. Sven had not expected to be spoken to during class by anyone except the instructor. He didn't know how to deal with it. It was like being back in elementary school. He decided to ignore it. He was nudged again.

"Yes, what is it?" he whispered, turning slightly towards his neighbor.

"I said 'Metaphorically if not literally' is what I said," this man repeated. He was a wiry little man with odd eyes—literally: one green and one blue. He had the broadest hands Sven had ever seen. His neck was like a turkey's.

"Please?" Sven said.

"Blind in act if not by nature," his neighbor grinned.

"Oh, yes," Sven said, not wanting to encourage further exchange.

But his caution was for naught.

"If you two continue talking, I'll be forced to separate you." The instructor had slipped into his bad-cop persona. Sven was mortified. His partner in crime just grinned. Slipping back into his good-cop self, their instructor, who had been, he had announced earlier, seventeen years with the CHP, proceeded into some statistics. Statistics and the anecdote—these were his weapons. Sven was prepared to admit that, coupled with his speech impediment, they were sufficient. He would never run a stop sign again. He looked at his watch. Fifteen minutes had passed.

It cost 100 million dollars a mile to build a freeway. By 2000 A.D., travel on the local freeway would have slowed to an average of 16 mph. There were 50,000 deaths a year from automobile accidents in the USA. Or was that just the drunk driving ones? Sven had lost track. His day at work had been a hard one. Now this. It had been a mistake all along to emigrate. He would have a nice house in Eskilstuna by now and three Swedish children. His wife would understand him, being a speaker of Swedish herself. He could go to soccer matches Saturdays. He would not have to work so hard, nor put up with the insane competitiveness of his fellow-workers. Everyone would be Swedish, except for some Turks and Italians and Asians. . . . Sven day-dreamed on.

Suddenly, people began to push back their seats and stand up. Some headed for the door.

"Ten-minute break," his neighbor said to him. "Say, I'm sorry I got you in bad with teach! Let me make it up to you. Have a cigaret." They were outside the building by now, and Sven shivered in the night air.

"No thanks. Don't smoke."

"Good for you." The little man lit up and inhaled ferociously. "That was neat about the Kleenex box."

"Please?"

"Guess you weren't listening. Can't say that I blame you. Does he have a voice-box or something in his throat? He told us that at 55 a Kleenex box could cut your head off. I like his taste in the macabre. I wonder whether a box of Q-Tips could do any permanent damage? My name's McPherson—Dan McPherson. I live right here in Santa Linda. Where you from?"

"Oh," Sven told him, "I live here, too. Though I am from somewhere else. From Sweden."

"Sweden—really? I used to live there myself. When I was a graduate student. I was in Comp. lit. Before I gave up language. Mycket bra. Hej så länge. Tjugo-fyra försupna käringar."

Sven laughed politely at this travesty of his native tongue. "You gave up language? That's not so easily done, I think."

"I used to write. Now I sculpt." The monstrous hands carved in the dark. "Sweden, eh? Had a good time there. Whereabouts?"

Sven named the little town not twenty miles from Eskilstuna. The man, curiously, had been there.

"My girlfriend then had a friend who lived there."

"I think it's time to go back in," Sven said, walking towards the door.

They re-entered the classroom. Everyone was sitting in the same seats they had sat in before. Now they were to see a movie. The instructor apologized in advance. It contained some gory scenes, he warned them, and they could close their eyes if they so chose. Sven thought this was contradictory. It allowed them to avoid part of the punishment. After all, everyone was there because of some wrong-doing. However, when the movie got to those scenes, Sven shut his eyes.

He was not surprised to find himself drifting down a river. He was in a small canoe. Where the paddle had gone to, who could say? The canoe was headed straight for some rocks. The sun was deliciously warm on his skin, and there was really nothing he wanted to do about the canoe. So he simply slipped overboard. He enjoyed swimming for a while and then his mother and his aunt Berit waded in and picked him up, wrapped him in a towel and set him down in the sand by the campfire. Here came his father, accompanied by sirens. The sun had set and a cold wind blew. He must have been sleeping because a small rock was digging into his ribs, had been, he realized suddenly, for some time. It was a drag. He would have to wake up in order to resituate himself. He opened his eyes and the lights were back on. Dan was poking him.

"You didn't miss much," he told him. "Time for another break."

Sven checked his watch. 8:15. Already he felt that he had spent most of his life here, at traffic school. But when he stepped outside, the dark silhouette of Santa Linda reminded him that he had another life. This rendered him almost loquacious with relief. "I don't know why I should have to see what happens when teenagers drink and drive," he said to Dan. "I'll never see forty again and I'm a member of A.A. All I did was run a stop-sign."

"That's what I'm in here for, too," Dan told him. "So's my friend Ace." He indicated with his newly-lit cigaret the balding haunted man coming towards them. He introduced him to Sven. "Another stop-sign-runner," he added.

"Yeah? Where'd they nail you?" Ace spoke in staccato bursts, intense and unsmiling. Without waiting for an answer, he went on. "They got me right here on this friggin campus. I teach here, y'know. It was a set-up. They've been trying to get even with me for years. Ever since I took em to court and beat the rap. They tried to get me for failing to yield. The cop was hundreds of yards from the intersection. He was in his own car, in plain clothes, on his way to work. When this guy started chasing me and high-beaming me, I figured it was some looney tune. The campus is crawling with em. It was nearly midnight. I'd just been to a movie. He must have radioed one of his brethren. They cut me off in a

155

real cop car. The guy was Martian. He was gibbering like a monkey. Ever since I beat the rap they've been laying for me. I could tell you things about the campus police that would curl your hair. It's like Central America."

Dan, unseen by Ace, adjusted a bolt in his own head with a finger. But this all struck a familiar chord in Sven. No doubt for that very cause, he took it with a large pinch of salt. "And how did they nail you eventually?"

"How? I'll tell you how. This cop hid in the dark outside the gates. You know, where the north road exits campus at the T-intersection with Paradise Way? Paradise Way is completely straight for half a mile in either direction. It was a clear night. No lights in either direction. So I slowed down, then speeded up as I went by the sign. That's when I saw the sonafabitch. Lights off. He knew I had an evening class. There hasn't been a cop car there at that time or any other since then."

"Why didn't you fight this one?" Sven asked him. "It is just his word against yours."

"Nine times out of ten, the judge'll believe the cop," Ace growled. "The other time, I had a friend in the car with me. Besides, you have to be at traffic court at 8 in the morning. I never get up before 9:15 since I heard that 3 times as many people have heart-attacks at 9 A.M. than at any other time. Traffic school is fractionally preferable to a heart-attack."

"Speaking of which, we'd better go back in," said Dan, who had been silent throughout the break, listening to his friend with a little smile on his face with its parti-colored eyes.

After you have between two and three drinks, Sven learned in the final (and longest) third of the evening, your eyes look in different directions. Even next day, for each drink you took the day before, your vision will be between 4 and 6% deficient. Sven was glad he hadn't known these facts back when he used to drink. He was sure they would have made him nervous and affected his driving adversely. He had actually been a better driver when a little looped. He knew a lot of drunks made the same claim. But in his own case, he knew, this had been true.

Sven hadn't stopped using alcohol because it impaired his driving, but because, Kathy claimed, it impaired his ability to communicate. Once he had a load on, he would lapse into Swedish. Kathy didn't know any Swedish, except for "Jag älskar dig," which, Sven had told her, meant "I love you," but she was pretty certain the words Sven kept uttering in his cups didn't mean that.

The instructor was calling for questions. A young man with a baseball cap and bushy back hair asked if it was okay to drive faster than the posted speed limit if there was no one else on the road. Then his companion asked if the instructor had ever, when with the CHP, pulled someone over for driving below the speed limit. This question interested Sven—it was one he had often asked himself. The answer was disappointing—it boiled down to "No." It was too difficult, the instructor claimed, to get by fourteen vehicles and reach the offending driver. Sven wondered why the amplified voice-thing couldn't be used: "WILL THE DRIVER OF THE RUSTED-OUT PICK-UP PLEASE PULL OVER TO THE SHOULDER." "WILL WHOEVER THE HELL IS AT THE FRONT OF THIS CONVOY PULL THE FUCK OVER AND COME OUT WITH HIS HANDS UP." These were just two of the sentences Sven had made up when caught in such traffic.

Unbelievably, it was time to go. He chatted briefly with Dan and Ace outside the building. They were all worn out but agreed to go for a coffee after the final class tomorrow night. This would give Dan and Sven time to advise their wives. They had both agreed with their mates that this was required. They laughed heartily when they found this out. "It wasn't always this way," Dan chortled. "There used to be spontaneity."

"Please?" said Sven.

"There used to be pleasing himself is what he means," Ace chipped in. "What I do. That's why I have no wife."

"Aha! But he has girlfriends," Dan put in.

"No, no girlfriends either." Ace sounded sullen. "I kept on pleasing myself, after the lights had changed. Now I have to please myself whenever I want. I might as well be married." But grumpy though he was, he agreed to come out the next night after class.

§

Sven arrived early the next evening. He wasn't going to take any chances. If he was late, he would have to repeat the 4 hours he had already endured.

The two young men who had asked the first questions the night before were chatting in the lobby.

"It was at Squaw Rock, late at night, and I was alone. Boy, next time! It's distance, time and space. Only if you accelerate fast enough. Front-wheel drive. . . ."

Sven thought to himself that they didn't sound chastened. But possibly they were, and this was mere defiance he was hearing. He smiled at Dan and took the empty seat next to him. Ace turned and waved. He was talking to a man Sven hadn't noticed before: a tall, thin fellow with gold wire-rimmed glasses and a goatee. He was about the same age as Sven and Dan. He was dressed conservatively. Everything about him looked buttoned-down. The instructor was in the same honky-tonk garb as last night. He locked the door and started, more or less, to speak.

They were shown a short film on seatbelts. Actors said various things about seatbelts. "I don't want to look chicken. I'm only going round the block. It's too difficult because I'm pregnant. I can't make this thing work." They received appropriate answers from a voice-over. "Al Unser doesn't go around worrying what his friends think. Most accidents occur within ten blocks of your home. You're playing Russian roulette with *two* lives now. Take time to read your owner's manual."

Someone was rattling the door, jerking it back and forth, kicking at it. The instructor opened it. A fierce large heavily bearded figure stood there, like Grizzly Adams. "You're too late. You'll have to re-register." The instructor spoke with complete authority. Sven held his breath—would the guy deck him? But he merely snarled and turned on his heel. The instructor re-locked the door. Now they could all feel more together, privileged to be permitted to attend. Sven wondered whether Grizzly Adams had been a shill.

But the adrenalin from this interruption soon ran its course and Sven felt himself flagging once again. He started recalling a code he needed to work out for a job his company had recently taken on. But he couldn't do it all in his head. He was reluctant to write. Dan had had his doodles confiscated yesterday. Unable to fill his mind with his work, Sven tried fantasy. But the attempt failed. Sven blamed the fluorescent lighting. Defenseless, he began to listen to the instructor.

When you went to a larger wheel and tire than the car was built for, your speedometer might be off by 8 to 16 mph, he learned. Actually, a speedometer isn't required by California law, he learned. There's a radar gun now that registers your speed as you approach even though the cop with the gun is headed in the opposite direction. In some places they automatically snap your photo and your license plate and the first thing you know that you've been caught speeding is when a citation with your snapshot on it arrives in the mail. How efficient, Sven mused. He himself always set his cruise control at the limit so that his foot wouldn't absent-mindedly cause his speed to creep up.

But during the first ten-minute break, Dan had another reaction. "Goddam 1984 mentality!" he exclaimed. "Secret surveillance!"

"Sure, that's how this society is run," Sven assured him. "Why are you upset? You sound surprised!"

Dan shot him a suspicious glance. "It wasn't always this way, Mr. Lindstrom," he said, at last.

"No, but surely, all of your lifetime," Sven continued, calmly. He had decided that if this man wanted to be his friend, he was going to have to be more than merely civil to him. He would have to level with him. "Why would you want to speed anyway? There's always the chance of getting caught, even without this latest technology. Just leave yourself more time to do things. Don't try to cram so much into one day. After all," he went on, seeing a way to appeal to Dan's good sense, "it's the society that tries to make you do too much. Why give it what it wants in the first place?"

Dan slapped Sven on the shoulder. "Makes sense," he said. "Okay, only two-and-a-half more hours. Let's go back in and take our medicine."

The second portion of the evening was to be enlivened by an exchange between the young man in the baseball cap and the instructor. The young man had had his feet up on the seat in front

159

of him, which was empty. (Presumably it had been meant for Grizzly Adams.) The instructor had requested that he remove them, citing the fire regulations. The young man then replied that the fire regulations must be a bunch of bullshit if they wouldn't let him put his feet up on the seat ahead when he wanted to. The instructor then gave the young man five seconds to put his feet down, or leave the room. Five seconds went by, and the young man failed to remove his feet.

"Okay. Out." The instructor hooked a thumb towards the door.

The young man put his feet down.

"Out, I said. Right now."

"Hey, I did what you told me. Where's the beef?"

"Where's the beef? I'll show you where's the beef. The beef is going to be right here if you don't vacate these premises right now. So git!"

Sven held his breath. He thought the young man was going to tangle with the instructor. But the moment passed. The young man strode to the door and flung himself through it. In dead silence, the instructor crossed to the door and locked it.

Sven felt bad. He felt the instructor had been dumb, to get himself into a no-back-down situation. Of course the young man was an idiot. But that was so clear, the instructor ought to have recognized the trouble he was getting himself into. The man was trying his hardest, now, to win back his authority, but the more good-cop he got, the smarmier he got, and the more obvious it became that he had lost it. Two people were taking notes, or doodling. One of the women began to buff her nails. Several people let their heads loll back, obviously sleeping. Several neighbors were whispering together. Dan nudged Sven.

"He just plain screwed up," said Dan, employing one of the instructor's favorite constructions. "He just plain blew it."

Improvising, the instructor elected to show the final film without a verbal set-up. Suddenly Sven and company were plunged into darkness and the film began rolling. It was called "Assault With a Deadly Weapon." Dan resumed whispering. "Only two hours and twenty-two minutes now. With two more breaks that leaves two hours and two minutes of class time. I'm really

160

looking forward to that cup of coffee. Only I think it'll be club soda. Ace wants to drink wine. So I said okay, let's go to Aloysius O'Toole's. You know that place?"

Sven said that he did. He didn't, but it was easier this way. When the time came to go there, he would simply accompany the others. He didn't want Dan giving him a description of a bar in the middle of the movie. Who knew? The instructor might turn mad-dog and order them out too.

Now Sven heard a motor revving up and then an almighty impact shook the room. Plaster fell from the ceiling and then a portion of the wall fell inward. The hole filled up with the hood of a Landrover. With an oath the instructor snapped the lights back on. The wall, being an outside one, had killed the vehicle's momentum pretty well, but it kept on slowly rolling forward, causing those seated in its path to scramble screaming and shouting out of its way. The Landrover, severely damaged, was wholly inside the classroom. A young man in a baseball cap slumped over its wheel. Several of his classmates, injured by flying bricks, sat on the floor, groaning, their hands to their wounds.

Confusion reigned. Sven felt guilty for letting his glance wander to his watch. This mess would take hours to clean up! He wondered whether it would be added on at the end, like injury time in a soccer match, or whether it was the sort of act of God that might count as substitute time. The instructor had unlocked the door so that one of the students could phone the police and Sven wandered into the hallway with Dan and Ace.

"I guess we have to stick around and be witnesses," Dan said. "But let's step outside where it's legal to smoke. That was a weird turn of events, wouldn't you say? I wonder if that completes the course? Neat, to end it with an object-lesson that way. I don't suppose the argument was a simulation?"

"I don't blame the little bugger one bit," Ace growled. "I'd have done it myself if I was twenty years younger. Only I'd have aimed better."

Sven wondered about Ace. He sounded like he meant it. And his tone didn't seem right, given that the driver of the Landrover might be seriously hurt. Nevertheless, he sat down next to him on a cement wall and carried on conversing while watching the police arrive, then the ambulance. He strained to catch Ace and Dan's remarks over the crackle of the police radios.

Ace was going on with his "twenty-years-younger" diatribe. The event seemed to have stirred up old feelings of rebellion. Ace was doing his best to turn it into an anti-war protest. "Those were the years," he shouted at Dan and Sven. "None of this trucking and higgling for a private good! We were selfless. We gave our lives to the Movement. We didn't think of things as owned—much less people. And past and future—we banished them from our minds. Past and future make cowards of us all! Do you think if that young man in the baseball cap had thought of the future, that he would have run his car through the wall of Babbit Hall?"

"Probably not," said Dan. "And then we would still be sitting in there, watching accident flicks. I see what you mean by selfless."

Sven thought that Dan might be employing irony. But it was so gentle as to go unnoticed. He supposed it all depended on the kind of relationship he had with Ace. "How long have you guys known one another?" he asked them.

"Half a lifetime." That was Dan.

"A lifetime." That was Ace. Together, then by turns, they told the story of their friendship: how they had met at graduate school at Berkeley, how they had moved to the country to live within a mile of one another, how they had seen one another through the breakups of their various marriages . . . "Ah, May," Ace wailed, "I never should have let you slip through my fingers!"

Dan played an imaginary violin. Ace played an imaginary saxophone. The harried-looking instructor approached their little group.

"You were members of the class, right? The police would like a statement from each of you. They're inside."

"How's the kid?" Ace asked, jumping off the wall.

"They think, broken collar bone, broken wrist, concussion," the downcast instructor replied. "I can't believe what he did. Anyway, I've got your certificates of completion in the room."

"I reckon we got an hour's-worth of demonstration, right?" Ace kidded the man. But the latter's gloom was impenetrable. Sven made up his mind not to slant his version either way. Poor suffering mortals, he thought. Besides, he disliked each of them about the same.

"No internal injuries?" Dan inquired, as they entered the classroom together.

"They don't think so," the instructor replied. "He was wearing his seat-belt."

Sven wondered if there had been a gleam of humor there. It was impossible to tell.

They waited until their statements had been taken, and then they walked out together. They decided it was too late to go to the bar. Then they decided that it wasn't. When they got there, several others from the class were there. One of them, sitting alone in the only available booth, was the buttoned-down character Sven had observed.

"Mind if we join you?" Ace asked, sitting down and gesturing to Sven and Dan to do likewise.

"I'm glad to tell you that you have," the thin man answered. "I'm called Brian. Brian Bartleby."

"I know you," Dan exclaimed. "You're the city councillor. The ecologically minded one. The *only* ecologically minded one."

Brian flushed faintly, with pleasure, Sven supposed.

"Really? A city councillor and you couldn't fix your ticket?" Ace = crass, Sven figured. But it was more of a disguise than spontaneous. In fact, his spontaneity felt like an act. He thought that Ace and Dan were like a bad-cop, good-cop team. They probably polarized this way in one another's company. Sven had noticed this phenomenon before between friends and couples. Now they were arguing over wine. Dan mentioned a name, and Ace clutched at his throat as though poisoned. The waitress appeared and Dan ordered that wine. Sven ordered a club soda. Bartleby was nursing a beer.

"Close call," he offered, amiably. "Missed me by two feet. Still doesn't seem real to me. Like something in a book. One of those flying-hamburger-stand novels. Oh yes," he went on, warming to his task, "I may be a city councillor, but I'm literate. And don't get me wrong. I may make fun of them, but I enjoy those American novels of the 60s and 70s. And was there an 80s? I understand that life is a core of unreality to charge its negative particles with the real. But you must understand I'm on my third

163

one of these, and like everybody else my age, I don't drink much any more. I once put away two bottles of Buena Vista Gewürztraminer with Theodore Thoroughgood. I put Odda Tala, the Finnish poet, under the table. However, I am out of training. But tonight's brush with oblivion has restored my sense of perspective. But you mustn't allow me to monopolize the conversation. Vera my wife tells me I do it a great deal. It was at her suggestion that I entered the political arena. She says I never use one word where three will do. We've been married 28 years. Twenty-eight years, man and beast! I was going to be an English professor, but the students couldn't get a word in edgewise. Talking is my one outlet. As you see, I'm a very uptight sort of person. I look like I've got a poker inserted in my hindquarters. Talking is my bohemian life, my *vie de bohème*. But you will find me a ready, if impatient, listener. Pray proceed."

But Ace and Dan were cracking one another up. Dan would say a line, then Ace would echo it, undercut it.

"I showed my son so many things!"

(A Beat)

"He made his father notice!"

(Four Beats)

"Dead night of the soul!"

(A Beat)

"Currently unemployable!"

(Four Beats)

"Save time!"

(A Beat)

"Kill it!"

(Four Beats)

"Currently unemployed!"

(A Beat)

"But helping keep wages down!"

Then they altered the mode slightly.

"Assault with a deadly weapon!"

(A Beat)

"The tongue of a traffic school teacher!"

Sven found it great fun. This is how it had been in his own youth, with mysteriously large dollops of leisure time, and he appreciated the nostalgia that was becoming immediacy right in front of him. He knew rules were there for a purpose, but that didn't mean he enjoyed keeping them. He was merely what is called stoical. Like Wordsworth, studied in high school, he knew the best has already happened. So he understood the various rages of the others, at this fact. Brian was proving unstoppable. He told them that he never went anywhere without Vera. If they wanted to know talkative, Vera was talkative. As for Dan and Ace, he said, three could play at that game, and proceeded to prove it, at least to his own apparent satisfaction: "The chicken and the egg! Things could be worse! The chicken and the soup! The cause and the effect! Exhibit A and B!"

But suddenly his mood turned. (He had had a fourth beer.) "Do you realize," he said, fixing each of them with a beady eye, the little beady eye, Sven thought, of a dormouse, "that while we sit here in jest, that poor youth lies suffering for our sins? No, I didn't like him much either, but still . . . What we can't bear to speak about, we will cloak in outworn tonal effects. Yes, I used to want to fill the libraries up with books, but now I spend all my time filling the meadows up with houses. Homes to you. All very ecologically sound, mind you. In the Greek, the root-word signifies—Waitress!"

But Ace and Dan wouldn't be bought another bottle of wine. "It's my ASS this time if they stop me on the road tonight," Ace complained. "God, I sound just like my Uncle Ed! Remember Uncle Ed?"

Dan did. "Round the bend, up your friend, in the end!" he chanted, doing a strange pirouette with one hand oratorically gesturing above his head. "Ace's Uncle Ed settled in these hyah parts," he explained to Sven. "We used to help him out."

"We helped him out a lot," said Ace. "We helped him out of the Main Street Saloon, we helped him out of there, and we helped him out of Aloysius O'Toole's, and we—we miss him, more greatness dead and turned to past, to leave us standing here blubbering."

"Blueberrying, that is, Ace. But it was blackberrying we used to like to do. Once," Dan went on, his face lit up, "we went out near Monte Nido. It was 104° in the shade. There was a creek nearby, with a little bridge over it. I went up on to that bridge and looked down, into about two feet of water. At least, I figured, I could roll around in it. When I got in, it was over my head! Everybody tore off their clothes and jumped in! It was so-o-o goo-oo-d . . .''

After the moment of silence Sven had remarked was obligatory, whenever some reference to the 60s of a possibly spiritual nature occurred, Ace spoke up: "I tell you, it's the memory of those times keeps me going now. There's little enough in the present."

"That's because the present is filled with work," Dan said. "Every month, everyone works longer, for less purchasing power. And there is no necessary end to this process."

"Yes, but it doesn't fill with work," Brian qualified. "It empties with work. This isn't your life's work you're talking about, this isn't a real way of life as in the phrase 'agriculture is more than just a job; it's a way of life,' this is nothingness filling up our world!"

Ace leaned forward and stared into Brian's face. After what felt like too long a wait, he said "Maybe."

After a further wait Brian said, "O I know, I go too far. When I sweep these statements around, I feel powerful. Like I'm making a clean sweep. If the worst has happened, things aren't too bad."

"That reminds me of a poem I once wrote," Dan said. "It was a collaboration. G. P. Skratz helped me write it."

"It must be quite long," Sven said, glancing at his watch. He had been having such a good time that he had forgotten to call Kathy.

"It's called 'The Blues,' " Dan went on. "It goes like so: 'Here you sit in the 13th century. And there's at least seven more to go.' "

"That Skratz is a funny man," Ace said. "What's he up to?"

"I don't know anymore, you know how it is. Poets speak to poets, sculptors speak to sculptors. Or don't speak to them. Anyway, I seldom leave Santa Linda, unless it's to go at least a thousand miles."

"Now I know who you are!" Sven told him. "You're Dan McPherson!" He wondered why he was so enthusiastic. He didn't

166

like Dan's work. But he liked Dan. Perhaps this would change how he felt about his work. But he didn't think so. Sven could tell that it was far out. Sven had *been* far out. But like most paranoid schizophrenics, he was a tad on the conservative side. Sven liked to joke that that explained the art scene in America. Or the literary scene. Or any scene that seemed appropriate. Sven, however, *knew* he was crazy. He stood up. Better go home.

"The trouble is," Ace was pontificating, "nobody dares to make a mistake anymore. So, nothing can happen. Nothing new. One ball and you're out. Two balls and you're having them *cut* out. It's the opposite of encouraging enterprise. When I first came here to teach, when it was time for the final exam we all drove to the ocean. We stood on the beach and they threw their final papers into the waves. If they washed back up, they got a B. If their papers sank or floated out to sea, they got an A."

"Ecologically dubious," said Brian.

"How come you don't do that these days?" Dan wanted to know.

"I give the students what they want. These days they want to be tested. So I test em. Tenure doesn't mean you can do just anything you want. The students pay our wages. We owe them our best imitation of their picture of who we are."

"That doesn't sound very spiritual-resistant."

"No. More like spiritless acquiescence," chimed in Brian.

"It was easier when everyone was spiritual," Ace muttered.

"Well, I've enjoyed a spiritual evening," Sven told them. "I have had much pleasure of your company, all of you. I hope we are meeting again shortly. Here is my card. And now I will say goodnight."

"Hold on, I'm coming too," said Ace.

And so, they decided, were Dan and Brian. The latter staggered slightly as they left. But it would be all right, he assured them. He was walking home.

They found out that his way led their way for part of the way. In the light of the February half-moon, the four of them formed an ambiguous silhouette, like the four heads of one monster, moving away towards the college parking lot together. There, their vehicles were waiting, like domesticated beasts. But they had a force not their own. They could only pray that their driver had been to traffic school over and over again, and kept his eyes on the road at all times. And plus which, that he was lucky. They agreed, these Hyundais and Lincolns and Toyotas and Volvos, these BMWs and Jags and Vettes, these Chevys and these old Dodges, silently, simply by being in juxtaposition with one another, among themselves, that all these things in one owner were too much to hope for. So the future looked bleak. This made the present all the more important. It was up to them to stop it from turning into the future—to delay that accident as long as possible. Breathlessly, they awaited the turn of the key in the lock.

AUTHOR'S P. S.

The Lid Off My Own Teapot

The teapot lid got broken today. We feel this evasive. Own the
responsibility! I broke the lid of the teapot today. You did so in-
tentionally? In one of your famous rages, no doubt—Where the
fuck is that objective correlative?! seizes the teapot, remembers
it cost 18 dollars, puts it down and hurls the lid instead. . . . Try
the middle voice: I let the teapot lid be broken today. Not bad.
But not good either. Do I really want to present a picture of a
man standing idly by while his own teapot lid breaks or gets
broken? You need to tell the whole story. "It's the first of October today, so I changed the calendar, that is pinned to the corkboard, which sits on the shelf—the narrow shelf—above the gas
stove, on top of which, the teapot. On the ledge with corkboard
and calendar: a (fairly heavy) can of Café Francais."

Meanwhile, she's gone into the kitchen and exclaims, "Hey!
What happened to the lid of the teapot?" And you can show her
this.

Printed August 1990 in Santa Barbara & Ann
Arbor for the Black Sparrow Press by Graham
Mackintosh & Edwards Brothers Inc. Text set in
Plantin by Words Worth. Design by Barbara Martin.
This edition is published in paper wrappers;
there are 200 hardcover trade copies;
125 hardcover copies have been numbered & signed
by the author; & there are 26 lettered copies
handbound in boards by Earle Gray each containing
an original drawing by the author.

Photo: James Garrahan

David Bromige grew up using the 16 Bus (London Transport) and the Bakerloo (London Underground). The first time he drove, it was a tractor with a load of peas on the rearload forklift which caused the front wheels to lift off the "ground" when he drove it up a heap of silage; because he hadn't approached the heap straight, and because he couldn't steer without those wheels, he went off the steep side through a barbed wire fence and over two drums of molasses. When he left the Berkshire College of Agriculture (by cloud) he gave some fields in Sweden a thorough harrowing but never drove a car (and then without license) until Saskatchewan. There was a spectacular non-fatal wreck (though without witnesses) out on the old Edmonton hiway. But that was someone else's fault. When he first got to Vancouver, he drove his sister's car around the block, and she got out at the first chance. Once, he borrowed his roommate's car, and the gas-pedal stuck to the floor. For a few months, whenever he was taken somewhere by car, he would curl up on the back seat in a tight ball of terror. Then he was introduced to tranquilizers. In Berkeley in the 60s, one required no car, being already here. When he moved to the country in Northern California like Dan McPherson (see within), he let his wife and others drive him around and around, until one got tired and shamed him into remembering. For 15 years now, he has had a current California license and he has a driving record his mother could have loved. He parks his car in the egalitarian lot at a California State University.